Dear Summer

SANTANA BLAIR

Chapter One

I hate summer.

I hate Concord.

I hate these awful popcorn ceilings.

Knocking over the pile of books that had been stacked and forgotten in the corner, he stretched his arms above his head. As he lay there in bed staring at the ugly ceiling, Parker Reeves concluded that staying three months in the room that used to be his father's office was going to a serious pain in more ways than one. The too small futon his body was uncomfortably draped across groaned in complaint as he shifted.

He also hated futons.

Ask any seventeen-year-old where they would choose to spend their coveted summer break and Parker was sure no one would choose the small town of Concord, Connecticut. So why on earth had Parker chosen to spend his break there with no proper exit strategy in place? Well simply put, he wasn't about to volunteer to spend the vacation time with his mother and her new husband on their summer long honeymoon. Unfortunately for Parker, those had been his only two options.

Hindsight being what it was, maybe he shouldn't have called his mother's bluff when she told him to straighten up and get his academic act together. Rather, he'd blown off the last half of junior year, only managing to pass with the bare minimum grades. As promised, his mother had thrown down the gauntlet and laid out his options. Frustrated with his mother, he'd packed his bags and hopped on a train to Concord, deciding a summer with his father would be the lesser of the two evils. After being in Concord for an hour, he quickly wondered if he'd made the wrong decision.

The quiet town was smaller than small and the most exciting thing they offered was their annual strawberry festival. Yeah, that pretty much summed up Concord.

Parker hadn't been back to the town since the day his mother had packed their stuff up into their Subaru and drove them away, leaving his father and the town in the rear-view mirror. Parker could be honest enough to admit he hadn't thought about either of those things much in the past seven years.

Of course, people would hear that and think it made him a bad son. Maybe it did. But he also thought those same people should know his father hadn't been so stellar about keeping in contact either. A workaholic professor was all Parker had known his father to be and the absence of his wife and son didn't seem to have incited any change. All that said, he and his father would now be stuck together for the next few months, whether either of them liked it or not.

So far, Parker wasn't liking it.

Still in bed, the constant hum of the oscillating fan that stood in the corner of the room kept his thoughts company. Then came the sounds of Luke clanging his way around the kitchen. The noise was an indication that his father had either forgotten about his presence, or that he simply didn't care. Not that Parker cared either.

From what he gathered over the past five days, his father's routine was pretty much like clockwork and he knew in just a few more minutes, he would hear the door open and close, followed by the sound of the car coming to life. Only after he listened to the car back down the driveway and disappear from the small cul-de-sac the house sat on, would Parker roll out of bed to wander through his day.

Rolling to his side, Parker unplugged his phone from its charger. He brought the screen to life, and almost immediately realized it was a waste of energy. Exactly zero messages from any of his so-called friends awaited his response. Their promises to keep in touch over the break had been made just as quickly as they'd been forgotten. His social life had begun circling the drain even before he'd left town.

Dropping his phone, he rolled his legs to the side of the bed, sitting up just as he heard the front door close. He figured enough was enough. Five days was going to have to be a suitable grieving period for the summer that could have been. Today, he would venture outside and try to find something, anything, to occupy his time in the microscopic town. If he didn't, he was quite positive he would die of boredom.

Grabbing the nearest and cleanest t-shirt in arms reach, he pulled the soft worn cotton shirt over his head. Leaving the room, he adjusted the waist band of his jersey shorts as he padded his way to the kitchen on bare feet. Ignoring the old fourth grade school photo of himself still held in place on the refrigerator, he pulled the door open and retrieved a bottle of water. Cracking the seal, Parker brought the bottle to his lips and drank the entirety in three big gulps.

It was still strange to find himself in a place that felt both familiar and foreign. Nothing about the kitchen had drastically changed over the course of the years he'd spent away. Parker had found it equally relieving and disturbing. The unchanged tile and cabinetry surrounded him as he leaned against the fridge, forcing him to feel the absence of his mother's off-tune singing as she prepared dinner for them.

He thought about finally answering one of his mother's many text messages. As frustrated as he felt towards her, he wondered if he could push it aside and let her know how things were going. The relationship had always been great between the two of them. At least they were until the last few years. That was when everything had begun to shift, her requests for him to stay focused in school began to sound less like the mother who loved him and more like that of a drill sergeant. Of course, it didn't get any better when Charles showed up and whisked his mother away into wealthy suburbanite life, subsequently casting Parker as the n'er-do-good step son. At least the role had come with the perks of a car... a car he was now also forbidden from driving until his grade point average matched his mother's standards.

He shook his head knowing he'd be relegated to using his bike upon his return home if he didn't muster the motivation to at least look at the books his mother had snuck into his duffel bag in hopes that he would buckle down over the summer. Problem was, Parker wasn't about to waste a summer doing the same thing he'd avoided doing for the past six months. Bored or not.

He pushed the idea of talking to his mother to the back

of his head, knowing if he did call her she'd have another lecture on the agenda for their conversation. Instead, he eyed the cash Luke had left on the counter with a sticky note telling him he'd be home late and that Parker should just order takeout for dinner. Thus far, Parker had only shared one awkward meal with his father since his arrival. Parker had eaten while Luke had stumbled around questions about Laura's new husband and Parker's life in New York, before he mercifully gave up and they finished their meal in silence. Cash and takeout seemed like much better meal options in Parker's opinion.

Yawning, he momentarily forgot about his plans to get out of the house suddenly feeling like a round of gaming and a nap would suffice for the day's activity instead. The new plan felt far more appealing and just as he was beginning to make up his mind, he heard the metal clang of a screen door followed by a series of grunts that floated through the open kitchen window from the yard next door.

He hadn't met any of the neighbors since he arrived, not that he expected his father to entertain much of a social life to even have friendly neighbors. Feeling curious, Parker crossed the worn tile floor, unlocking the patio door and sliding it open giving himself a clear view of the neighboring yard. He watched the source of the noise, a barefoot girl, doing her best to drag a large cardboard box across the rich green grass in the direction of a shed.

His offer to help her disintegrated somewhere in his throat as he tried to get a glimpse of her. Her strawberry blonde hair fell over her face in a soft curtain, keeping his attention in demand until she grunted in frustration and stood upright, planting her hands on her hips as she seemed to reevaluate her technique. Parker inadvertently took a step, wanting to get a closer look at the girl who might be the salvation to his summer.

Before he could open his lips to introduce himself, her head dipped once more as she reached into the box and pulled out a Polaroid camera. She had snapped his picture before he even knew what was happening and then turned on her heel and disappeared into the shed. Abandoning the box in the middle of her yard, she closed the door behind her with a definitive slam.

His hope of having some fun with someone in his social age bracket was fading fast. Not many could rebound from creeper status. Still he found it hard to pull his eyes away from the shed. Questions began sprinting through his mind. Who was that girl? What was she doing in that shed? And what was she going to do with the picture? Not wanting to look any more foolish than he had already managed to, Parker retreated into the house and away from any more unsuspected camera lenses.

Parker's curiosity tagged along like a faithful companion as he collapsed in front of the television, breakfast now forgotten. He powered up his game console with thoughts of the girl next door filling his mind. He fought temptation to return to the kitchen where he would be able to catch another glimpse of her. Instead, Parker gave his undivided attention to his game play even when he heard her return to dragging the box.

As the day spiraled into evening, Parker stayed out of sight. Ignoring another two calls from his mother, the only social interaction he managed to engage in for the day was his reply to his father's text message that he'd be home later than originally anticipated (big surprise) and the call he'd made to finally order himself a pizza. When the doorbell rang and pulled him out of his worn in seat on the couch, Parker had presumed his food had finally arrived.

Parker had presumed wrong.

Pulling the door open, he was greeted with an image of

himself. A Polaroid snapshot had been taped to the front door. A simple message had been scrawled in loopy cursive beneath the captured image of his shocked face.

Take a picture, it lasts longer.

Chapter Two

By the time his father left for work that morning, Parker had already showered and dressed. Wanting to make a better impression this time around, he had spent half the night planning out what he was going to say to the girl next door. She'd already busted him as some weirdo-peeping-tom-creep and the stakes against him were already high.

Parker paced the floor a dozen or so times as he waited for the clock to announce that it would be socially acceptable to pop up on his neighbor's doorstep. When a final glance at the clock on the stove told him the time had come, he had no sooner put his hand on the door to open it when he heard his neighbor's screen door squeak open and swing shut. Without waiting around this time, Parker immediately headed her way. His slow jog immediately caught her interest caused her to freeze in place, as she watched him ignore any trespassing rules by hopping the low dividing fence.

That soft red hair of hers rippled in thick waves that shone almost golden in the sunshine. She lifted a hand to shield her light brown eyes illuminated with amusement and question. The bridge of her nose and her cheekbones were sprinkled with a dusting of cinnamon freckles against her creamy French vanilla skin. Something about her instantly knocked him off-kilter, and the rehearsed introduction he'd spent hours perfecting was ripped from his mind and scrambled under her gaze.

Parker offered her a smile that he tried to keep friendly. He was just meeting the girl, no need for her to know how desperate he was to have someone to hang out and commiserate with.

"Hey, my name is Parker. I live next door."

"You live next door?" Her forehead wrinkled in confusion. "How come I've never seen you around here before then?"

Ah, so they were jumping right into the interrogation portion of the introductions.

"Well I don't really live next door..."

"But you just said you did."

"I know. Bad word choice." Parker ran a flustered hand through his sandy brown hair. "I'm, uh, staying with my-uh, Luke for the summer."

Her cocked eyebrow challenged him for more information. Her light brown eyes and their tiny flecks of green slid over him in perusal, that gaze of hers once again tilting his axis.

Clearing his throat, Parker shifted his weight from one foot to the other as he tucked his hands into his pocket. That was when he finally noticed the wrench and bicycle tire she held in her hand, his brain gratefully finding an exit to the conversation about his father.

"Can I give you a hand with that?"

"I don't know, can you?"

She gestured to the worn and broken down frame of a bike leaning up against the mysterious shed she had disappeared into the day before. Once upon a time, it was probably a nice bike, maybe even functional. Now? Not so much. There wasn't a wrench in the world that would restore it to glory.

"Yikes."

"So I guess that's a no then." Dropping the tool and tire to the grass, she walked in a small circle, apparently reevaluating whatever it was that she needed the bike for.

"Hey, does Luke have a bike?"

"I wouldn't know. I guess we could check the garage. What do you need it for?"

"Because." She grabbed hold of his elbow and pulled him in the direction of the fence. "I'm going to learn how to ride a bike today."

"Wait a minute!" Parker's feet stalled, eliciting an eye roll and impatient huff out of her.

"I don't have all summer, Parker. You can ask questions while we look for a bike."

It was kind of funny to think how his hating being told what to do had landed him here in Concord in the first place, yet here he was being cajoled through the yard by a girl who hadn't even told him her name yet.

Using a rough assumption, he guessed she was at least sixteen. Her slim figure was partially hidden underneath the oversized, long sleeve, navy blue tee shirt she wore; her suntanned legs bared by the frayed denim shorts her legs stemmed out from. In her bare feet, she showcased ten toes in lime green nail polish and a toe ring that kept catching both the sun and his eye every time she shifted her feet.

Making their way back over the fence and around the house to the garage, Parker paused at the door.

"What's your name?"

He crossed his arms. This time he purposely waited to hear her response, making sure she wouldn't skirt around his question.

"Excuse me?"

"Your name. You never told me your name."

Her face softened with a genuine smile. "Oh, sorry about that. My name is Summer."

His own smile grew. "Nice to meet you, Summer."

Opening the door, he ushered her in before him. Finding the bike was far easier than he anticipated due to the meticulous order that his father kept the garage in. It had taken only a minute before they spotted several bikes hung on the wall.

Parker lifted them off the hooks with ease. After examining them for a moment, he picked one and set it on the ground between them. He quickly checked the brakes and tires, grateful to find them both in working order. "This is about the right size and should do the trick. Why don't you go get some sneakers on and I'll see if I can find a helmet around here."

Summer waved his comment away. "I don't need a helmet."

"Um, yeah you do."

She chortled. "Who are you? My mother?"

Embarrassingly enough, he realized he did sound like a mother, his in particular.

"Look, you need a helmet. I've never taught anyone how to ride a bike before and I don't need to have you getting a concussion on my permanent record."

Summer smirked in amusement. "Who said you were teaching me how to ride?"

Shrugging a shoulder, he grinned. "I guess I did."

She seemed to mull it over for a second before giving a nod of acceptance. Skipping away from him, he could only hope she was in search of shoes and a helmet. Turning his attention back to the bike, he heard her voice as she called out over her shoulder.

"Little kids do this all the time; how hard could it be?!"

"You better not let me go until I'm ready."

Parker studied the way her knuckles had begun to turn white as she gripped the handlebars. Tendrils of hair escaping the old baseball helmet he had demanded she wear were now darkened with perspiration. Now that he had declared it was her turn, her fiery determination to ride the bike now flickered with insecurity.

"I won't let go. I'll keep my hand right on the seat until you get going."

She wet her lips with the tip of her tongue. "I'm serious, Parker. None of the sneaky letting go mess that puts kids in therapy later, wondering why they have trust issues."

"Summer," he stepped around to the front of the bike straddling the tire between his legs. "You got this."

With one last nervous exhale she gave him a firm nod. "I got this."

Parker steadied the bike as she placed one pink Converse covered foot on the pedal, readying herself for the ride. She took off slowly, Parker easily keeping up alongside her. As promised, his hand gently held onto the back of the seat as she gained both balance and confidence. As she did so, Parker felt his own smile grow as his hand eased away.

"Summer?"

"Don't let go, Parker!"

"I already did."

"Parker!" She wobbled with her exclamation, but just as he expected she quickly righted herself. Circling the cul-de-sac, she pinned an angry glare on him. "I'm going to kill you when I get off this thing."

Her threat was lost as she beamed a smile his way. Parker may not have understood why she had never learned to ride a bike before then but her smile was enough to convince him that he didn't care.

"Grab the camera, Parker! Take a picture!"

He had wondered why she had returned to the lawn with sneakers and a camera in hand. Grabbing the camera from where it lay in the grass, he made a note to add it to his growing list of questions.

Lifting it to his eye he caught her in the viewfinder. The expression of pure joy and accomplishment practically made her glow. The look on her face was more than he had ever expected to see and knowing he had a part in putting it there did more for his spirit than anything ever had.

Parker jogged out of the street before taking a seat in

the grass of his front lawn. Pulling his knees up and resting his arms across them, he watched her lap after lap. Her confidence growing with each pass she made until she used the brakes exactly the way he showed her. She swung her leg over the bike, wheeling it back up to his driveway and leaning it against the opened garage. Tossing the baseball helmet to the side, she joined him in the grass taking a seat off to his right.

With her face flushed, her chest rose and fell as she took in deep breaths. "That's the best feeling in the world."

Parker gave her a sideways look. "I think that may be a bit of an exaggeration."

She turned her face up toward the sun, she shrugged a shoulder at him in response. "Did you take the picture?"

"Mmhmm. I think you were a bit too preoccupied yelling at me about letting go to notice."

"Which reminds me..."

Parker was hit with a handful of grass as she giggled and rolled out of his retaliatory grasp. "You asked me to teach you how to ride a bike. Well I did, didn't I?"

Summer rolled to her belly then, now resting on her forearms. "Did your dad teach you?"

Parker didn't comment on her dad reference, choosing to nod instead. It had been one of the very few times he could remember actually having a fun time with his dad. He felt the thoughts darken his mood. He shook them away, refusing to let the day turn so fast. "Can I ask why you never tried to ride a bike before?"

Summer seemed to sift through her words before looking his way again. "When most kids were learning how to ride bikes, I was in the hospital. I couldn't do much of anything while I recovered and I had to stay inside a lot. By the time I could get back to the things that other kids were doing, I think a part of me was just scared to try…"

"Until now." Parker finished her sentence.

She grinned gratefully. Parker watched as Summer studied the now perfectly developed photograph. Traces of happiness were etched around her eyes.

"What are you doing later, like around five thirty?"

Parker thought about the empty house awaiting his return. "I'm doing whatever you have in mind right now."

"My mom isn't going to win Top Chef anytime soon, but she can make a good lasagna. You should come over for dinner… if you want to, that is."

Lasagna sounded better than any takeout leftovers he had waiting for him in the fridge.

"I'll be there."

Chapter Three

Wanting to make a good impression on Summer's parents, Parker made sure to iron his best shirt before he got in the shower to get ready. After hearing she had spent some time being really sick as a kid, he began to think she probably had some protective parents, more so than the typical teenage girl. The last thing he wanted was for them to think of him as some bad seed kid. Plus, he could only imagine what kind of impression his antisocial father had already given them. If they forbid her from hanging out with him, he would be right back where he started.

Bored, alone, and on that stupid futon.

Leaving behind the emptiness of his father's house, he quickly jogged down the steps and crossed the lawn to Summer's house. The house seemed to be architecturally similar to Luke's, but that's where the similarities ended. Summer's home was painted a rich shade of blueish gray, the bright flowers bloomed in pots on the front stairs complimenting the deep goldenrod yellow color of their front door.

He rubbed his palms across his pants before knocking. It took just a moment before he heard footsteps drawing near. When the door swung open, he was greeted by a familiar smile on a new face. The woman, who he naturally assumed was Summer's mother, had the same soft eyes and nose as Summer; her hair a few shades lighter and pinned up in a clip.

"You must be Parker. I'm Kelly, Summer's mom. Please come in out of this heat."

Parker shook her hand and accepted her invitation as he stepped over the threshold. If the outside of her home screamed happiness, then the inside of it whispered love. The positive energy seemed to instantly surround him felt nearly palpable.

Tucking his hands into his pockets, he glanced around trying to take in any and everything that could give him clues about the kind of girl Summer was. The pictures on one wall captured her life in snapshots, while another wall held pictures that hadn't put her in front of lens but seemed reminiscent of her still.

"Did Summer take these?"

Kelly looked at the collection he indicated. "Yes, she did. Wow, you have a good eye."

"She's good."

Kelly gave the pictures a tender look before waving for him to follow her as she walked towards the kitchen. "I tell her the same thing all the time. But you know, I'm just the uncool Mom, so what I say doesn't count. Anyway, make yourself comfortable. We still have a little bit of time before dinner is ready. Summer ran out to her shed, she'll be back in just a minute. We can chat while we wait."

Parker swallowed as he took a seat at the small kitchen table. Moms had this supernatural ability to say the most innocent things that made you feel the weight of every wrong thing you had ever done come back and land squarely on your chest. He could only pray Summer would be back in time to rescue him.

Drying her freshly washed hands on a clean towel she turned her attention to the salad she was preparing. "Summer tells me you're Luke's son. It's so good to finally meet you. He's mentioned you often."

Parker wanted to scoff at her polite lie but he didn't. Instead, he gave her a nod. "I am."

"It's so nice to have another young person in the neighborhood. It's so quiet and peaceful here we thought the change would be great for Summer, and I think it has been, but I'm afraid that she's been stuck with just us old folks for a few years now."

"Have you and your husband lived here long then? I don't remember seeing Summer before we moved away."

Kelly shook her head. "From what I've gathered, you had been gone for a few months when we moved in."

Parker's next question fell away from his lips as Summer came through the patio door. Her damp hair pulled into a messy bun on the top of her head, she wore a long sleeved black tee shirt with a pair of faded cropped jeans, barefoot once again.

"You can stop talking about me now, Mother."

"And how do you know I was talking about you?"

Summer grabbed a cucumber slice from the cutting board, smiling brightly just before she popped it into her mouth. "Because I'm your favorite topic of conversation."

"Wash your hands and pretend like you have some kind of home training in front of guests!" Kelly protested as she playfully pointed in her daughter's direction.

Summer pressed an exuberant kiss to her mother's

cheek en route to the sink. Parker thought of similar moments with his own mother, his phone suddenly feeling like a brick in his pocket.

"Parker, would you be a darling and pull the lasagna out of the oven? You can grab the oven mitts there on the counter."

Parker hopped into action, grateful to be doing something that made him feel of use. The smells hit his nose as he pulled the door open causing his mouth to water. He carefully slid the pan out, placing it to rest on top of the waiting cooling rack. Once he was done, Parker joined Summer in setting the table, the both of them sharing a smile as he placed three plates on the table.

"Will your husband be joining us for dinner?"

It was Summer's turn to snort in inappropriate laughter as Kelly drew in a sharp breath. "No. It's just us."

The look that passed in Summer's eyes made him want to know more but he was smart enough to leave it alone. Even if Summer would be willing to talk about it, everything about the thin smile Kelly now wore told him she wasn't.

"Let's eat then."

They did just that.

For the short while that followed, Parker didn't think about school, his parents, or even his amnesiac friends. For the time he spent with Summer and her mom, Parker remembered what it felt like to just be happy.

After Kelly packed a Tupperware container full of leftovers for him, she shooed them out of the kitchen. Taking the glasses of sweet tea outside to drink on the patio, Parker was grateful his evening wasn't quite over yet.

"Your mom makes a great lasagna."

Summer's lip curled into that sugary sweet grin of hers. "I told you!"

Curiosity getting the better of him, Parker set his drink down on the patio table turning to face her. "What grade are you in?"

She shook her head as if she didn't understand the question.

"Grade, as in school, what grade are you in?"

"I'm not. I graduated a couple weeks ago in May."

"What?!" Parker sat up straight in his chair. "How old are you?"

"I'll be seventeen in a month. I was homeschooled ever since second grade and just ended up graduating early."

If only Parker had been so industrious. He wasn't looking forward to another year of monotony. Thinking of all the unread school work and college brochures that sat back in his room, he felt the weighty voice of responsibility tugging at the back of his mind and it sounded an awful lot like his mother's voice coated in disappointment.

"Lucky you."

Summer harrumphed, mixed emotions clouding her face. "Can I show you something, Parker?"

Parker nodded. Standing, he followed as she led him down the two small steps and across the yard in the direction of the shed. Pulling a small gold key from her pocket, she fit it into the door of the shed, unlocking it before pushing the door open. Instead of the dusty storage area he expected to find, he was surrounded by a well decorated space. Sunshine yellow walls were decorated with thinly wired white tree lights. Large throw pillows and bean bags making the room even cozier, while Polaroid snapshots brought life to the walls.

"What is all of this?" His awe weighed down his words

and eliminated any chance of him playing the cool aloof guy.

"It's a Me-Shed. I got it last year for my sixteenth birthday. It's basically a tree house on the ground. I come out here when I want to do my own thing or I just want some privacy."

"I bet you could throw a decent little party in here if you wanted."

Summer threw him an incredulous look before rolling her eyes at him. Parker bit back his amusement, his eyes pulled towards the large corkboard mounted on the wall, and the now notorious Polaroid camera hung from a nail beside it.

Drawing closer he took in the banner pinned across the top, the words The List written in Summer's loopy cursive handwriting. Two pictures were pinned under the banner; one was another picture of him in all his dazed and confused glory when she caught him spying on her, on this picture, she'd written a different caption.

Meet someone new.

The other pinned picture had been the picture he'd snapped of her earlier as she rode a bike for the very first time, just as she had captioned it.

"What's the list?"

She reached into the back pocket of her jeans and pulled out a folded piece of paper, waving it in his direction before tucking it back into its place. "It's a to do list for me, full of things I've never done and things I want to do before summer is over."

Parker felt his brows furrow a bit. "Like a summertime bucket list?"

She shrugged her shoulders. "I guess. Every day I am going to do at least one thing from my list, and I will take a picture of it so I can add it to my board."

"Pics or it didn't happen." Parker lifted the camera from its resting place. He turned it over in his hands a few times. "So, when do we get started on the rest of this list then?"

"We?" She took the camera from his hands, rehanging it on the wall. "I didn't ask for your help."

"I know you didn't, but look at it this way, I could be like, your official liaison to all things summer. I've already helped you with your first two things."

"I don't think so, this is a personal thing."

He watched the way her lips pursed around the word personal to make sure he knew exactly what she meant. No worries there. Everything about this girl seemed to push Parker right back into his place if he dared toe the line.

But this felt different. Parker remembered how it felt to watch her face come alive as she took off on the bike all by herself that afternoon. It had felt good. It felt like he had done something worthwhile with his time. It was a good feeling and he wanted more of it.

"I'm going to be stuck next door all summer anyway, I could help you out and you could make the summer a little less miserable for me. Everybody wins."

Summer didn't answer, instead rubbing her palms together. "I'll think about it."

It wasn't the exact response he wanted but it was one he could work with.

Leaving the shed, the sun had just begun to take its final bow for the day. Summer walked him across the yard towards his fence, stopping first to collect his Tupperware container of leftovers.

"Thanks for having me over. It was nice."

"Thanks for coming. It's been a while since we had a new face at the dinner table."

Reaching the fence, they both paused. The sound of crickets actually chirping reminded him he should say something to end the awkward silence that stretched on.

Summer cleared her throat. "Well, I should get in the house."

Parker nodded, not wanting her to go but also not knowing how to make the moment last. Finally, she turned away from him and began her return. Parker crossed the fence heading to his own door.

"Hey, Parker!"

Her voice stopped him in his tracks. He spun around to face her, question in his expression.

"I thought about it. I'll see you tomorrow... that is, if you're still interested in helping me?"

Parker shook his head in humorous disbelief. "Oh, I'm definitely interested."

"M'kay." She caught her lip between her teeth as if he couldn't see she was smiling. "Goodnight, Parker."

They walked backward, keeping each other in sight as they drew farther apart.

"Sweet dreams, Summer."

chapter Four

When Parker woke the next morning, he had no idea what he was in store for. None of the scenarios he ran through his head had prepared him for the sight of Summer sitting at the dinette set in his kitchen. She sat there looking quite at home in her plain white tee shirt and pink denim shorts. Tie dyed converses on her feet and her hair captured into two braids, she looked ready for an adventure.

"Are you really in my kitchen right now?"

"Finally!" Summer stood with exasperated satisfaction coating her smile. "I was beginning to think you had entered into hibernation or something."

He crossed his arms over his chest, all of a sudden keenly aware that he was shirtless. "How are you in my kitchen right now?"

"Luke let me in on his way to work."

Parker's eyes widened. "He did what?"

Ignoring him, Summer held out a toaster pastry. "Here,

you should hurry up and eat. Your sleeping in has put us behind schedule."

Pulling his phone out of the pocket of his mesh shorts, he checked the time. "It's barely ten thirty."

She rolled her eyes. "I've been up since six."

"Why?!" Parker nearly choked on the idea of waking up early for no reason.

Not surprisingly, Summer ignored the question, instead cocking her head in the direction of the now illuminated screen of his phone. Parker quickly hit the ignore button sending another call from his mother to voicemail before tucking it away again.

"That was your mother, shouldn't you take her call?"

"I need to get dressed, I'll call her later."

Parker took the pastry from her hand turning to head back to his room. Summer followed on his heels. "Or you can call her back now, I can wait."

"What happened to the girl who was just berating me for being late? Don't we have a list we need to be getting to?"

Summer leaned against the open door frame. "If you only answered questions the same way you ask them."

He laughed. Grabbing her hand he shook it once, "It's so nice to meet you Pot, you can call me Kettle."

"Touché."

He stared at her for a moment before clearing his throat. "Um, Summer?"

"Yeah?"

"I'm going to have to take my shorts off in a second so..."

Her cheeks flushed with color as she spun around. "Oh God! I'm sorry. I'll go... Come over to my house when you're naked, I mean, dressed."

Parker watched her retreat down the hallway before allowing the laughter that had been collecting in his chest to escape, admitting to himself that Summer looked really freaking cute when she was embarrassed.

When Parker walked up the steps of Summer's back porch he found the patio door open. He knocked twice before popping his head through the doorway to find Kelly leaning on the counter reading mail and sipping a mug of coffee.

She waved him in with a smile. "Good morning, Parker! I hope Summer didn't wake you, she's been a bit eager to head out."

"No ma'am," Parker stepped fully into the kitchen as he returned her smile with one of his own. "She waited until I woke on my own before berating me for my life choices."

Summer's eyebrows slammed together as she entered the room from steps that led upstairs. "Well excuse me for not wanting to waste a perfectly good day by sleeping. Not all of us can afford to luxuriate in laziness."

Parker feigned hurt. "Ouch!"

"Summer!" Kelly chastised. She gently swatted her daughter's head with the papers she held. "Excuse my daughter, Parker. I swear she has manners. She must have left them in her other pair of pants."

Summer stuck her tongue out at him.

"Alright, I'm off to work. You two have fun today. Be safe. Don't do anything illegal."

"Yes, ma'am." They replied in unison.

Kelly deposited her mug into the sink and grabbed her bag off the island. "Summer, I'm working late this evening. Dinner's in the fridge, just pop it in the oven when you're ready. Call my cell if you need anything."

Summer's eyes rolled upward. "Mom, I know!"

Kelly cringed. "I know, I know. Sorry!" Kelly pressed a kiss to her forehead. "I love you."

"Love you too."

Kelly took several steps towards the door before pausing. She turned to Summer, her "mom-face" firmly set in place. "Make sure you take-"

He watched the way Summer's playful face turned somber, her voice dropping to a low whisper so he couldn't hear her response as she shifted away from her mother's touch. He wondered if it was because she didn't want him to know whatever it was that they were discussing, or if she just didn't want to be discussing it at all. Having spent the better part of the last twenty-four hours around Summer had already taught him she liked to play her cards close to her chest.

Kelly gave Parker's arm a gentle squeeze as she headed out the front door and left them alone for the day.

"What kind of work does your mom do?"

"She's a stripper."

Parker's jaw dropped before he could stop it. He tried to say something but found himself stammering his way through various vowels.

"Oh gosh, Parker. Relax, it's a joke. She's a nurse."

"Well your mom is hot so I wouldn't go around joking she's a stripper, it's not that far-fetched of an idea."

"Um, ew." Summer tossed him a dirty look he quite enjoyed. Twice so far that day he'd already thrown her off her game, and he was beginning to realize that getting under her skin was pretty entertaining. There was something captivating about the way all of her emotions shone through on her face. That same special something about her was what kept him entertained and had him more intrigued than ever. He decided not to test the limits of her patience so early in the day, instead deciding to pursue another avenue of discussion, mainly, what the heck they were doing that day.

"I have two questions."

"Only two? Somehow I find that hard to believe." The playful glint had returned to those molten honey tinted eyes of hers and he felt something in his chest tense up.

"What are you packing in the bag, and do I need bail money?"

"I made us some sandwiches earlier. I figured after we climb the tree down by the creek, we can have a picnic lunch."

Parker had very few memories of the town but he did vaguely remember a tree by the creek. He remembered the massive trunk and wide twisted branches. It had been a monstrous site for a kid with an active imagination, and something about the way Summer's eyes were lit up with excitement told him that not much had changed since he'd been gone.

"Climbing a tree, I assume that's on the list."

She gave him an affirmative nod. "And having a picnic. Today, we cross two things off. I have to run upstairs for a second, will you fit this blanket in the bag for me. We can get going in a minute."

Under a perfect blue sky, they walked to the creek, enjoying the break in humidity the day's weather gave them. It was a perfect day for a picnic and once again Parker found himself grateful for Summer's plans that had gotten him out of the house. Until he saw the tree.

The tree seemed twice as big as he remembered. Its branches extending like gnarled limbs over the lush green grass and calm waters of the creek. The song of the cicadas was a melodic reminder that there was no one around to save either of them from a broken neck.

"Are you sure that you want to climb *this* tree?"

"Yep, positive." Summer walked around the trunk of the tree twice before sliding her back pack from her shoulders, letting it fall to the ground. "Give me a lift?"

"This tree is huge!"

"Go big or go home. Lift, please."

Going home sounded like a great option to him. "You know, I might start to feel offended you only keep me around to do your bidding."

Summer cut her eyes at him. "I do not. Now help me up... please."

Biting back his grin, he dropped his bag alongside hers. Interlocking his fingers to serve as a foothold, he stooped to give her a boost. With her lean legs and his height, she easily reached the first branch and pulled herself up.

The girl who wavered in trepidation before her first bike ride ever was nowhere to be found as he watched her fearlessly scale and climb the branches.

"Summer!"

Too busy disappearing into the branches, she didn't bother answering. The occasional flash of color from her sneakers was the only way of knowing she wasn't stuck somewhere.

Parker contemplated his next move.

He thought about climbing up after her. That was just before the other part of his brain chimed in with a reminder he wasn't as fearless as he would have liked to believe.

"Parker!"

Summer's voice rang out loudly in the air. He scurried around to the other side of the tree, the sight of Summer nestled casually in one of the higher branches was enough to make the blood rush to his head. "Okay, you can come down now."

"Come on up, Parker! You have to see this!"

"Uh, that's all right. Maybe next time."

"Don't tell me you're scared of heights."

Heights weren't the only thing he felt scared of at the moment.

There was something about this girl being that high up with no decipherable fear that had his insides knotted up. "Just come down Summer, I'm starving."

She shook her head, "Not until you take the picture."

Right. The photo. Scrambling back to the bags, he rummaged through their lunch items before pulling out the camera. The faster he took this picture, the faster she could begin her descent. Finding her once again sitting at ease, he aimed the lens in her direction. And then, like the brave lunatic he was discovering her to be, she stretched her arms wide.

"I'm flying!"

She was fearless and innocent and it took his breath away.

"You're going to be falling in a second!"

With her feat captured, he held his breath as she made her way back down just as stealthily as she had climbed. Reaching the lowest branch again, Parker drew closer and helped her hop down safely. Her cheeks were pink and flushed but shone brightly with the joy of another accomplishment.

He had been so ready to take her to task over the risky stunt, but seeing how happy she was took all the wind out of his sails. Instead, he just handed her the picture and her camera before laying out the blanket for their picnic.

Summer took her spot on the blanket, kicking her sneakers off to the side. Digging into her bag, she handed him one of the sandwiches. "It's turkey. Can I ask you something, Parker?"

Taking the sandwich gratefully, he met her gaze. "You always do."

"How come you didn't answer your mom's phone call this morning?"

Parker should have known she wouldn't have let it go so easily. Still, the question caused his heart to twist a bit tighter. "I guess I don't have much to say to her these days."

"But she's your mother." Her forehead creased with worry and question.

"I know who she is. I also know she's off on some honeymoon adventure with her new husband and I'm stuck here..."

All by myself. He left that part unsaid.

Everything about her demeanor screamed that she didn't approve of his answer. He didn't feel like explaining things to her. He busied his mouth with a large bite of his sandwich, hoping she got the hint.

"My dad left us three months after we found out I was sick. I haven't seen him since."

Summer's unprompted revelation was coated in a softer sympathetic tone that caused him to freeze mid chew. His eyes focused on her stoic face. To someone with an untrained eye she hid the emotions well. But he knew the feelings that were there; those feelings were old friends of his.

"What a piece of crap."

She nodded almost absent mindedly as she pulled the crust from her sandwich. "That's putting it lightly."

Chapter Five

Parker found himself walking a bit slower as they drew nearer to their homes. His body seemed to be having a subconscious reaction to the idea of parting ways with her. They had spent the better part of the afternoon under the shade of that old tree. As much as Summer could push him with her questions, she also had an uncanny ability to make him feel at ease. That ability only seemed to grow with every moment they spent together. Their time spent eating and cloud gazing had been no exception.

He waited until she unlocked the front door and pushed it open before he slid the now lighter back pack from his shoulders. Clearing his throat, he extended it her way. "Here you go. Thanks again for lunch."

She gave him a quizzical look as she took the bag from him. "No problem."

"So maybe I'll see you tomorrow, I mean-"

"Parker." Summer held up a hand. "When my mom said she left dinner in the fridge she also meant it for you."

Parker ran a hand over his face, a lame attempt at covering the smile that instantly came with her invitation.

"Oh! Well I guess I can join you... I'll just have to move some things around in my schedule."

Summer shook her head in amused annoyance, her eyelashes fluttering as she rolled her eyes at him. "Oh, right, I'm sure."

Parker followed her as she walked to the kitchen. Pulling out a rectangular glass pan from the fridge, she nudged him with it.

"It's no five-course dinner but I hope you'll like it."

"I like food." Parker supplied. He took it in his hands, though not quite sure what to do with it.

"Well, that's a win for you then. I've got to run upstairs and..." her words trailed off.

"What do you want me to do with this?" He held up the lasagna, hoping he didn't look as pathetic as he felt.

Summer's forehead wrinkled in question. "Turn on the oven and pop it in. There's probably a note on the stove with the temperature and time because, well, my mom just has to be my mom at every possible chance."

Spinning around, he spotted the pink square sticky note stuck right under the digital time. In the second it took him to do that, Summer had used the distraction to escape upstairs before he could ask her anything else.

Curiosity hung in the back of his mind as he carefully followed the reheating instructions. His culinary skills were limited to sandwiches and all things microwaveable and while his appetite was eager for him to throw the pan in the oven, his cautiousness came from a desire to avoid burning Summer's house down in the process.

By the time Summer rejoined him, Parker had forgotten all about her quick exit and was now focused on the delicious aroma beginning to fill the kitchen. His stomach rumbled in approval as he pulled the oven door open.

"You know it will cook a lot faster if you stop opening the door every two seconds."

He ignored her, instead feeling the heat wash over his face as he inhaled. "It smells amazing. What is it?"

Summer gave him a bemused smirk as she opened the fridge and pulled out a bowl of salad. "Easy there, it's just a chicken casserole."

"I've never had one."

"Never had a casserole? Really?" Her lips twisted in disbelief.

Parker shook his head honestly, closing the oven door gently.

"I've had too many to count. It's sick kid syndrome. Every time I'd go into the hospital, we'd end up with a freezer full of casseroles. Between my mom's practicality and the neighborhood's generosity, I'm kind of a casserole expert."

Parker grinned. "Oh yeah, so you're a bike riding, tree climbing, casserole expert who likes to take pictures of unsuspecting nice guys."

Summer tapped her chin with one of her slender fingers. "Hm, I'm not sure I like what you're implying there. As I recall, you were spying on me..."

"Spying is kind of harsh, I'd say I was intensely observing your activities."

She laughed then. One of those truly hearty laughs he

couldn't help but smile at. "I stand corrected then. The food should be just about ready now, let's get our plates and we can eat in the TV room, it's almost time for Jeopardy."

Summer handed him a plate and ignored the look of amusement he was sure he wore. "Jeopardy? As in the boring game show? I'll take reasons why Summer doesn't have a social life for six hundred, Alex."

Summer cut her eyes at him. "Oh well excuse me, Mr. Popularity. Feel free to call up some of your friends to hang out with you instead—oh wait..."

"Ouch."

And there he was, put right back in his place.

Dinner was a comfortable affair, somehow made more complete with the addition of the two of them yelling out responses along with the TV contestants in between bites of food and sips of iced tea. Summer's apparent competitive nature drove her to give him her best version of a smug smirk every time she answered correctly. Her undeniable good heart kept her from laughing at him every time he answered very incorrectly... which was a lot.

The girl knew her way around obscure trivia that was for sure.

Parker dropped his fork to his empty plate. "So, when are you going to let me see that list of yours?"

"My list? Um, I don't know, I hadn't thought about sharing it with anyone, really."

Summer didn't look at him as she replied. She kept her face focused on the screen of the TV but he could see the reluctance instantly color her face.

"I just think I might be able to better help you out with some things if I know what those things are ahead of time."

"I know." Her hesitation hung there in the air long enough for him to guess what she'd say next. "It's just kind of personal."

Parker wasn't going to push the matter. As curious as he was and as eager as he was to help her out, he wouldn't bully her into his way of thinking. Not that Summer would ever stand for that to happen anyway.

Returning her attention back to the television, the lips she had been rolling together in contemplation now relaxed as she seemed to forget about his request. He took her non-committal answer for what it was and followed suit by turning back to the end of the game show.

It wasn't until the credits had begun to roll that Summer spoke again as she held her cell phone in his direction.

"Can I get your phone number?"

Parker ignored the unexpected jolt he felt in his gut as she asked him. "Uh, yeah, sure."

"It will be easier to just text you instead of popping up in your kitchen waiting for you to wake up every morning."

"I'll set an alarm for tomorrow, just text me later and let me know the plans."

"Will do."

Parker heard the familiar sound of his father's car pulling into the cul-de-sac then, a heaviness suddenly pulling at him. He stood collecting their plates.

"I should get going but I'll help you with the dishes first..."

"Parker, they're paper plates, I think I can manage."

Summer stood alongside him, taking the plates from his hand, her other hand giving his shoulder a squeeze of encouragement. "Go on, I'll text in a bit."

Leaving Summer and her house that felt like home behind, he slowed his footsteps as he neared the house he dreaded. His father paused just as he placed the key in the lock of the door.

"Parker?"

Unsure of why his father felt the need to add the questioning inflection to his name, Parker felt his own response add a bit of a bite to its tone. "That'd be me."

Parker had always resembled his father and as he looked over at him now, it was one of those moments where Parker felt like he was looking at a future version of himself. They had always shared the same muddy brown hair and hazel eyes, but in the last few years as Parker had grown well over his mother's head it had become abundantly clear Parker had also inherited the genes for his father's height.

He came to a stop a foot away from where his father stood in front of the still closed door. Luke seemed to mull over what he wanted to say to fill the silence of the awkward space they seemed to naturally orbit in.

"Your mother called me."

"Oh really? That was nice of her."

Parker stepped past his father, reaching around him to turn the lock and open the door. He had diligently worked at avoiding a conversation with his mother and the second to last thing he wanted to do right then was to have the conversation vicariously with the father who hadn't ever really been much of a father to begin with.

Luke followed him into the house, setting his bag down and locking the door behind them.

"Parker, hold on a second."

Parker paused and gave Luke his best imitation of a patient look. Luke placed his bag down, dropping the pile of mail onto the small nearby table. "Laura, your mother... She'd like you to call her."

He knew that already. "You can let Laura know I'm fine."

So now his mom had answered his silent treatment by going to Luke for answers. Apparently his sporadic one-word responses to her frequent messaging wasn't going to suffice. On one hand, it surprised him. It had been quite some time since his mother had displayed such an active interest in his daily life. But then he would think back a few years and remember the way it used to be between them. When he did, it all made more sense. His mom had been the consistently reliable rock in his life for years. Where Luke always seemed to come up short, she'd stepped in to fill the void. She was the single person in his life who he never had to worry about leaving him hanging.

Until she left him hanging.

When Charles swooped into their lives and began to wine and dine his mother, he'd been okay with all of it at first. He had felt grateful his mom had met someone who made spending time with her a priority. But then the casual dates became fancy gala dinners and weekends spent traveling to and from places became Laura's norm, while Parker was left behind.

The mom who had always asked him about his day and insisted they talk had morphed into a mother who left sticky note reminders of his to do list.

When her love life took him out of Brooklyn and away from the life he'd built with close friends, she hadn't asked him how he felt about any of it. He'd been plopped down in Long Island, enrolled in a prep school, and given a monthly allowance by his step-father to pacify him. When his discomfort gave way to poor decision making, she talked at him instead of to him; listening had been a long-forgotten option.

So, there he was with his life rapidly souring, his mother was living the sweet life, too blinded by her own happiness to notice, and his father was long lost in a world of academia. His life was taking a nosedive and since both of his parents apparently had better things to do with their time, he decided to just enjoy the ride.

Parker rolled his eyes. Of course, she wanted to talk now.

Luke's voice pulled him out of the whirlpool of thoughts he'd been sucked into.

"She mentioned that you have some thinking to do about colleges and I thought if you need any help maybe I could lend a hand. Maybe you'd like to come to campus one day and take a tour, you could even audit a class or two, I could make a call-"

Parker's frustration simmered just under the surface of his skin. His ears grew hot and his head buzzed; he wondered if it was possible for pent up emotions to cause a brain aneurysm.

I don't need you.

He cut his father off. "I don't need your help, Luke."

Luke's mouth opened and then closed before he nodded. Parker didn't wait for anything else before he turned on his heel and retreated to the privacy of his room.

For the first time since he'd met Summer, he found himself lying in bed, wishing he was anywhere but there.

Chapter Six

After his conversation with his father, expecting a text from Summer had fallen to the corner of his mind. With his frustration still simmering, he felt happier than he expected to be as he saw the phone number with the unfamiliar area code asking if he was asleep yet.

Parker chuckled as he checked the time.

Parker: Um it's not even ten o'clock. I'm seventeen not seventy.

Summer: And the mystery of why you sleep your days away is finally solved.

Parker: I have to bank up some beauty sleep. All of this isn't just genetics and good luck you know

He could almost see her smirk as she bit back yet another witty reply. Instead of the text message response he expected, he was caught off guard as his phone came to life with an incoming call from her.

"Hello?"

"So about tomorrow." Summer gracefully leaped past all courteousness as only she could do. "I want to go to New Haven and go to the art gallery."

That sounded boring. Then again, boring with Summer never actually felt that way, probably because she was involved. Doing nothing with Summer was more fun than doing anything without her. "Okay, and how are we getting to New Haven?"

"That's what I'm calling about because I don't know. My mom has to go into work too early for us to ride with her."

"We could always use an Uber. I have an account."

"Uber? You want me to get into the car with a stranger? How about no?"

Parker almost laughed aloud at the incredulity he heard in her voice. He wondered if he should point out the fact that just a couple of days ago, they hadn't even known each other's name. Not wanting to press his luck, he kept the remark to himself. "Come on Summer, everyone uses it now. What's the worst that could happen?"

And then for the next fifteen minutes Parker was subjected a list of all the various worst-case scenarios Summer had ready to go, including but not limited to the probability of being kidnapped by a serial killer.

"I thought this was your summer of yes, trying new things, and all that jazz."

"I am saying yes to the things on my list, but I'm saying no to being some headline in the evening news."

The girl who had scaled the monstrous tree so fearlessly and laughed gravity in the face just hours before had been replaced yet again. This was the second time he'd seen her be so intimidated by something that felt a bit mundane to himself. Summer was a riddle, and he was determined to figure her out. Parker stood and walked over to the window wondering if he could see her room from his own. The lone light in an upstairs window gave him the answer he wanted.

"Summer, come to the window."

"Why?"

"Because I'm asking you to."

He heard her grumble and sigh but then just as he hoped she would, she appeared in the window looking confused.

"Okay, why am I at the window Parker?"

"Look down." He waved to get her attention. When she spotted him, he liked to think his near perfect eyesight had caught a smile playing on her lips. "Just like I asked you to come to the window, I'm asking you to trust me on this whole car situation. I'll set it up and I'll make sure we get there safely. I got you, Summer. I promise."

And he meant it.

It was right then that he fully realized how deep he'd gotten himself in with this girl. Parker had always been the kid who didn't even want a pet because just the thought of the responsibility that came along with it always felt stifling. But for some inexplicable reason, he was willing to commit himself and his summer to this beautiful enigma of a girl.

Everything he knew about Summer so far told him she was the type of girl that was made for something special; that she was the type of girl who would float rather than fly if given the chance. The fact that life hadn't always allowed for her to explore that, made him more determined than ever to erase every uncertainty weighing her down. Parker hoped his words would be enough.

More than that, he hoped he would be enough.

"I trust you, Parker."

Those four words were still bouncing around in his mind, echoing as he watched her exit her house and cross the front lawn the next morning. He'd set no less than seven alarms to ensure he would be on Summer's timetable for the day's adventure. His mind and body had rebelled against the early wake up but her wariness from the night before was enough to remind him he needed to do everything in his power to make sure the day went as smooth as possible.

That meant he needed to get his butt out of bed on time.

Any residual complaint his body was hanging onto was instantly vaporized when he laid eyes on her. The baggy scooped neck tee she wore with her denim shorts showed a little bit more skin than he was accustomed to her revealing, but still leaps and bounds away from the stuff some of the girls back home would wear. The fact that she didn't seem to care much about her clothes beyond the fact of them being clean was refreshingly relatable. Her wavy golden red hair shone in the morning sunshine and was held away from her face by a thin headband. Excitement and trepidation were battling for prominence on her face just before she spotted him ready and waiting for her. A shadow of relief overtook her face then.

"Nice shoes." His smile came fast and furiously as the mismatched pair of pink and black Converse sneakers she wore drew her nearer.

Summer's lips curled up at the corner as she took the seat next to him on the porch. Stretching her suntanned legs out in front of her she crossed her ankles and wiggled her feet happily. "Don't be jealous, I was born this cool."

"Somehow I don't doubt that one bit."

"So, when is this car coming?"

Parker noted the suspicious inflection in which she coated the word car. He bit back a chuckle. "I just sent in the request. Elliot and his car should be arriving in about ten minutes or so."

"Elliot." Summer pursed her lips around the word, as if she could taste his entire moral compass in the three short syllables. Coming to some secret conclusion, she twisted her perfectly pink lips to the side and reached into the small bag hung across her body. It was only when he heard her asking him how much the ride would cost did he realize she was reaching for her wallet.

"Don't worry about it. Keep your money."

"What do you mean, don't worry about it? It's my plan, the least I can do is pay for us to get there. I'm not going to take your money."

"I'm giving the money to Elliot, not to you. My account is already linked to a credit card. It's taken care of."

Parker could see another probing inquiry forming in her mind but the arrival of their car pulled her attention from the question of his level of privilege and focused it back to whatever serial killer theory was running through her head at the moment.

To her credit, when Parker stood and extended his hand, Summer immediately took it and pulled herself to her feet.

"Let's get to it then."

Fortunately for all of them, their driver turned out to be a young college kid on break for the summer and Summer quickly pulled him into a conversation of something so extremely dull and educational that Parker couldn't even pretend to understand. Instead, his mind focused on the way she took the seat closest to him, the warm skin of her thigh pressed against his own. His nose was filled with the pleasant scent of her peppermint shampoo. His eyes seemed to constantly stare at her lips every time she ran the tip of her tongue over her bottom lip before she talked, which was a lot.

Now Parker wasn't looking to make this thing with Summer any more than what it was. But as a seventeen-year-old boy with a working set of eyes, a raging set of hormones, and a ridiculously cute girl in his company... he was keenly aware of the fact that things happen.

"Wow."

The simple word encompassed all his feelings. There was just something about the architecture of the buildings surrounding them as they walked along the sidewalks in downtown New Haven that reminded you of the history these streets were steeped in. It wasn't anything like New York City, but it was a special place in its own. The variety of cultures that were woven into the tapestry of the city and its famous university probably had a little something to do with it.

"I haven't done this in years. I'm excited."

He was too, but the rules of playing it cool meant he needed to keep his enthusiasm at an acceptable level. He clapped his hands together and rubbed them vigorously,

"So what's our story?"

The look of happiness on Summer's face quickly pixelated with question. "What do you mean?"

"I know the whole visit to the art gallery is your list thing, but I thought we could add a fun layer to it with an idea of mine."

"I'm listening."

"What do you say we play tourist and create ourselves a little backstory? Something a little bit more exciting than we drove over from Concord for the day."

He could see her thinking. It was the whole wearing her emotions on her face thing again. Hopefully she wasn't thinking his idea was lame because now that he said it out loud he was starting to think that maybe fun wasn't the first word to come to mind.

"I'll be Lucy..."

"A red head named Lucy, how original."

She ignored his gentle teasing. "From Delaware."

"That is the most random choice."

"Don't criticize my fake life choices!" She flipped her hair over her shoulder and gave him a cheeky grin. "Okay, your turn."

"Jean-Pierre from Aruba, but you can call me J.P."

Summer's giggled practically exploded from her lips. "And you called me random!"

Parker was proud of the response he'd elicited. "Don't laugh at J.P. He's an avid traveler who loves going from port to port on his yacht, enjoying his life of leisure with the companionship of his many female admirers."

Summer just laughed harder. "Now *that* is the funniest thing I ever heard. You and female admirers. Poor J.P. is delusional from all that sun he gets on his yacht that must overcompensate for... something."

"Whoa, easy there Luce, no need to play dirty just because my back story is better than yours."

With the laughter still dancing in her eyes, Summer linked her arm with his, tugging him. Together they climbed the steps and entered the art gallery. Parker had been mentally prepared to be bored out of his mind, quite sure that his only reprieve throughout this trip would be teasing Summer.

Summer quietly led them to the first section where she took her time observing each piece before moving to the next. Parker dutifully followed behind her, watching the curiosity twinkling in her eyes, wishing he could read her mind

"What part of New York are you from?" Summer's hushed question came as they wandered through the spacious room.

"We lived in Brooklyn up until last year, we're in Long Island now."

One of the richest counties in Long Island to be exact but he left that little tidbit out. Right now, Summer didn't need to know about his mother off living her version of a Cinderella story.

"Do you like it there?"

Parker shrugged a shoulder. "I liked it in Brooklyn."

"So, you moved to Long Island because of your step-father and you hate it. Is that why you're in Concord this summer?"

"I don't recall saying all of that."

"Lucky for you, I happen to be a spectacular listener. You don't have to say it for me to hear it."

Parker smiled despite the turn the conversation was taking. "I'm in Concord because I had no other choice. For the second time in my life I was given the choice between my mom and my dad. This time I chose Luke."

Rounding a corner, Summer steered him to one of the available benches sitting in front of one of the paint splattered canvases. She took a seat and patted the spot next to her inviting him to do the same.

Of course, he took the seat next to her. This girl had this way about her that made him want to do whatever she wanted. It was terrifyingly intriguing.

"What made you choose Luke this time?"

Parker had asked himself the same question about a thousand times since he informed his mother of the decision.

"My mom made me really mad. Choosing to come here was a way to let her know that she wasn't my favorite person at the time."

Summer rolled her lips together for a moment. It was a clear sign she was about to hit him with a whammy of a question. He braced himself.

"Why?"

It was the single most complicated question she could ask.

"It's complicated." It was an honest answer but Parker knew it wouldn't satisfy Summer.

"That's the funny thing about life, most things are."

Miraculously, she dropped the subject and for the next hour he followed her around the gallery listening to her talk about artists and something called the abstract expressionist movement. Parker really tried to make sure he paid attention, because hanging with Summer might actually teach him something, but then he would get distracted by the way her breath would hitch at the sight of what looked like splattered paint.

"How do you know about all this stuff?"

Summer smiled at him cheekily. "Jeopardy."

"I'm starving."

Parker stretched his arms as they stood in the warm sunlight. Their gallery tour and Polaroid documentation complete, they now had no plans for the afternoon. He didn't know how Summer felt but he was in no rush to head back to Concord.

His eyes fell on the line formed at one of the several parked food trucks just down the block. Long lines meant good food. Parker's stomach rumbled in anticipation.

"Let's grab lunch from that food truck over there."

Summer's face fell at the suggestion. "You want to eat street meat? Is that even sanitary?"

"One, I don't think I like the term street meat. Two, it's a food truck. It's a thing, and a completely sanitary one. I promise."

He could see the hesitation pulling at her and instead of waiting for her to find a reason to shoot the suggestion down, this time he grabbed her hand and gently tugged her along as he made his way to the line.

Parker scanned the chalkboard menu hung on the side of the truck as they waited there turn. "Is there anything you don't eat?"

"Um yeah, I don't eat from meat from the street."

Parker ignored her grumbling and stepped up to order. Keeping it classic he ordered them both two classic New York style hot dogs and a couple of bottles of water. Handing her the food, they walked to an empty bench that offered plenty of shade while they ate.

"This is probably the best thing I've ever eaten."

Parker smiled proudly watching her chew in delight. It was so completely satisfying to watch her find such enjoyment in eating that for a handful of moments, he forgot all about his own food.

Taking the camera from where it sat between them, Parker snapped a shot of her mid chew with her cheek smeared with mustard and her face covered in bliss.

"Ew, that's the worst picture ever!"

She was so wrong. Parker slid the picture into his pocket and got busy with his own food.

"Tell me something I don't know about you."

Summer wiped her mouth with one of the paper napkins as she chewed thoughtfully. "I was a vegetarian for a few years."

Judging by the way she went in on the hot dog, Parker could safely assume she was a happy carnivore again. "What changed your mind?"

"Bacon. Nothing tastes like bacon and I had to ask myself would I want to live the rest of my life never tasting that again."

"Poor little piggies." Parker shook his head in mock judgement before taking another bite of his hot dog.

"What about you? Tell me something I don't know."

"Contrary to you, I live a fairly boring existence. I usually just hang out with my friends when I can."

"Tell me about them."

They're a bunch of traitors. "I'd rather not."

She frowned at him. "You don't want to talk about your mom, you don't want to talk about why you're here in Concord... you don't want to talk about your friends. This is becoming a bit of a one-sided friendship, Parker."

"I just don't want to ruin a good day right now. Ask me anything else and I promise I'll answer."

Summer placed her food down beside her, turning to face him. "How did things go last night with Luke?"

Dang it.

He narrowed his eyes at her Cheshire Cat grin. "It went badly, which is the better than I expected it to go to be honest. My mom called him and asked him to talk to me, but it was only about college stuff."

Summer waited expectantly.

"He offered me to come to campus and audit some classes this summer."

Summer perked up. "That's awesome."

"It's the worst idea I've ever heard."

Her forehead wrinkled in concern. "Why? You're going to be a senior next year, you'll have to be applying to colleges pretty soon."

"I'm not going to college, and even if I did go, I definitely wouldn't go to one where I'd have to share a campus with Luke."

"Even if by going to that college you'd get free tuition?"

"I don't care about money." Parker struggled to keep the edge out of his voice. "That man spent my entire life choosing his job over me. I'm not going-"

Parker's words were washed over with the current of emotions. This is why he didn't want to talk to her about this.

"I don't want his help, Summer."

Summer's hand found his and gave it a gentle squeeze. "I hear you."

He didn't doubt it. With all her relentless and probing questions, Summer may have single handedly been the most persistently nosey person he'd ever met. But she was also the only person who ever asked him a question about his feelings and then actually stayed quiet long enough to hear the answer. It was a show of genuine care and Parker hadn't felt cared about in a long time.

"I'm in Concord because I blew off school this past year." His brain shoved the words out of his mouth before he could reconsider the decision.

Questions danced in her eyes as she stared at him. "What do you mean you blew off school?"

"I skipped classes, didn't turn in any assignments, failed some important tests... toss in a handful of detentions and a suspension and I think you'd get the whole picture. I pulled some good final grades out at the end of the year to pass but my GPA is crap now. My mom tried to do some scared-straight-tough-love type of thing. But I wound up here. Now she's trying to get Luke to sway me to a life of academia."

Summer's normally readable face was absolutely still for a moment.

"Alright then, I'm going to help you."

Parker's head was already shaking as she finished speaking. "Absolutely not. I don't need help."

Not from his mother. Not from his father. And definitely not from Summer. He was already trying his best not to look pathetic in her eyes, having her see just how far he'd let himself fall wouldn't do him any favors.

"Everything about your situation begs to disagree."

On his list of things he didn't want to do, arguing with Summer and dealing with school were probably in the top three. He was becoming a master at avoidance but she had a steely look of determination in her eye that told him she wasn't going to be letting this one go.

Summer stood collecting her trash and throwing it into the nearby garbage can in a huff of frustration. "Don't be an idiot Parker, don't sit here and piss your life away to teach your parents some sort of backward lesson."

"Why do I need help? Why can't I just live my life?"

"You have opportunities some kids our age would love to have..."

Parker rolled his eyes, "You sound like my mom."

"Well, your mom sounds like a beautiful and intelligent woman then."

Parker bit back his smile. Instead of looking at her, he picked at the label of his now half empty water bottle and made a great show of examining the nutritional label. If he looked at her, he was doomed.

"What if I told you one of the things on my list was to help someone? If you let me help you with this, then you'll still be helping me with my list... which you already agreed to do and I know you wouldn't go back on your word."

Catching sight of Summer's smirk was enough to cause an involuntary smile of his own. He should have known that by telling her the truth about his summer in Concord, she would decide to rescue him from his own self-sabotage.

And because she was Summer, the crazy bossy but undeniably cute girl from next door he couldn't say no to, he was probably going to let her.

"Thanks for everything today, Parker." Summer spun around to face him as they stood on her front porch. After an afternoon playing tourist around downtown New Haven, they finally made their way back to Concord just in time to watch the moon's arrival in the dusky sky.

"I had fun." He offered her an honest and timid smile.

"So-"

He held up a hand to interrupt her. He already knew what was coming and this time he was ready for her. "Fine. I'll let you help me."

Summer's excited applause came just before she attacked him with a ferocious hug. "I'm so happy! You won't regret this."

Little did she realize, regret was the last thing on his mind right then. With her arms snaked around his neck, he was too busy filling up on the crazy good feeling that came from being hugged by her. It was a feeling he wouldn't soon forget even as she released him.

"Tomorrow we'll start. We can focus on my list during the day and then after dinner we can study together."

Parker couldn't help but chuckle. "You've been formulating a schedule the whole way home, haven't you?"

"Maybe." Her eyes told him a different story. "Will you wait here for a second? I want to give you something before you go home."

He gave a quick glance in the direction of his home with the darkened windows before nodding his head in agreement. The moment she disappeared through the door, he took a seat on her front porch watching the lightning bugs come out to play. Realizing he hadn't even bothered to check his phone with the exception of arranging their transportation for the day, he pulled it out of his pocket and began an aimless scroll through his Instagram timeline.

Snapshots and videos of his friends celebrating nothing in particular greeted him. The lack of his presence seemed to have absolutely no effect on their lives. A few days ago, it would have sent Parker on a passive aggressive commenting spree. But now, he liked a few of the pictures before sliding the phone away. It was kind of funny how quickly things changed.

The sound of the screen door opening announced Summer's return. She plopped down on the step beside him before handing him a single key hung on a simple leather string.

"What's this?" He turned the key over in his hand for a moment before noticing the sarcastic look brewing on her face. "I know it's a key. I mean, what is it for?"

Summer smirked, "It's for my shed. I thought you might like to have somewhere to go whenever you need to get away. The key will let you in even when I'm not around."

"Going somewhere?"

She gave a gentle shake of her head. "Just take the key and say thank you."

He realized the depth of the gesture. As promised, Summer had listened to both his spoken and unspoken sentiments. He hung the key around his neck. "Thank you, Summer."

Bumping his shoulder with her own, she gave him a soft smile. "See you in the morning, Parker."

chapter seven

When Parker woke before his alarm went off that morning, he couldn't deny the effect Summer was having on him. He didn't see any point in trying to fall back asleep, knowing even if he succeeded, Summer would show up and drag him out of bed if she had to.

Leaving his bed somewhat regrettably, he made it through his shower with no sign of her on his doorstep. Back in his room, he pulled on a pair of shorts and a tank top, slipping his feet into a pair of Vans while pocketing his cell phone. Grabbing a pack of toaster pastries, he headed out of the door crossing the yard to locate his budding partner in innocence.

Parker had decided the whole upside to this waking up early and having Summer tutor him for the summer was gaining more time with her. Summer was unlike anyone he had ever met and though he might have started hanging out with her out of social necessity, it had almost instantly become so much more.

His hand found the key hung around his neck, bringing

the memory of the shared moment back to the surface. He didn't know such a simple gesture could mean so much to him that he'd think about it for half the night. But it had and he did.

"Good morning, Parker!" Kelly's cheerful chirp greeted Parker as he neared the back porch where she sat, sipping her mug of coffee in her pajamas and slippers.

"Morning." Parker offered a bright smile in return. "Is Summer awake? I brought her breakfast."

He held up the foil wrapped package and elicited a hearty chuckle from Kelly.

"I think she just hopped in the shower. She slept in a bit today, you two must have had quite the adventure yesterday."

"I learned a lot, that's for sure."

"She had a good time. That makes me happy." Kelly's tender smile was glazed over with an emotion he couldn't quite pinpoint.

"I did too. I really did."

Her smile dipped a bit at the corners. She cleared her throat and lifted the mug to her lips as she took a moment to take a sip. "Do you want to sit and wait for her? I have a fresh pot of coffee if you're interested."

"As tempting as that is, I think I'm just going to head over to the shed and wait for her."

If she was surprised Summer had given him a key to her shed, her face didn't show it. She smiled, this time happily, before telling him that he was welcome to join them for dinner later and instructed him to make sure he put sunblock on.

Moms just gotta mom.

In the quiet of the shed, Parker used the moments alone, to thoroughly take in the space. Since he'd seen the space last, she'd added the new photographs to the wall, including the one of her mustard stained face. She must have stolen it from his pocket sometime after he had hidden it away yesterday.

He made the mental note to add stealthy pick pocket to his *"Everything I Know about Summer"* list.

Taking in the empty space of the board he wondered about what lay ahead of them. He so desperately wanted to see that list of hers. Trying to be patient as he earned her trust was more than important to him, but it didn't erase how much he wanted to know.

Perusing the small bookshelf sitting in the corner he pulled a paperback book from the shelf. The cover was worn and bent in several places, all the signs of wear and tear pointing to a book that held a story about its reader as well. Taking the book and collapsing into the empty bean bag chair, he turned to the first page and began to read.

Summer came through the door later than Parker had expected her to. Her hair was still damp from the shower and she had pulled on a long sleeve white and black Nike shirt that hung so long on her frame it almost covered the black shorts she wore. Most of the girls Parker was used to hanging out with capitalized on every opportunity to flaunt their cleavage, so Summer's demure choice of tops wasn't lost on him. Just as much as he noticed her apparent refusal to show any skin on top, his eyes were drawn to her basically bare legs.

Summer had some really nice legs.

"Sorry I'm late."

She collapsed into the bean bag that sat unoccupied to the right of him.

"No biggie. I was just reading this book. I hope you don't mind." He felt a flash of inexplicable embarrassment as he admitted how he chose to spend the time.

She glanced over at the spine of the worn book and smiled gently. "I don't mind at all. That's actually one of my favorites. My mom read it to me when I was sick in the hospital and I've read it so many times I've lost count."

Parker closed the book, rubbing his thumb over the cover of the book and imagining a little Summer curled up with Kelly reading the story of a special friendship.

"Would you mind if I borrowed it? I know it's a kids book but I've never read it and I'd like to finish the story."

Summer nodded and her smile grew deeper. "Of course you can, Parker."

"Thanks." The embarrassment slowly faded away as he placed the book to the side. Finishing the story would have to wait for now. It was time to get on with the day's agenda, and on the top of that plan was whatever she was ready to scratch off her list next.

"What's the plan for the day?"

Summer pulled her hair into a messy bun using the elastic she wore as a bracelet most days. "Let's go pick strawberries. Newton Farms has open pick time today."

Parker couldn't remember the last time he picked his own fruit from somewhere other than the produce drawer in a pre-stocked refrigerator. "I'm down."

"And we're riding bikes over to the farm."

Parker feigned a shocked face. "Whoa, look at you, hitting the road again!"

Summer rolled her eyes in amusement. "Today we hit the road and the farm. Tonight, we hit the books."

He wished he could say he'd forgotten about the newest little addendum to his summer plans. But ever since she appointed herself his tutor, it had been the only thing he could legitimately focus on. Deep down Parker knew he would have to get his act together sooner or later. He just didn't expect it to happen with Summer at the helm.

But then, maybe that's what he needed to get his act together. Her bossy nature was counterbalanced with her pure intention and good heart, plus she was really something to look at. Summer's beautiful but bossy nature might be exactly the thing he needed to motivate him to do the work he'd been blowing off for far too long. He was kind of eager to find out.

"I know, I know." Parker came to his feet and extended a hand towards her. "Ready to go?"

She answered when she slipped her hand into his and allowed him to lead them out of the shed. With her hot pink Converse sneakers already on her feet, this time Parker only had to deal with Summer fussing over the necessity of wearing a bike helmet.

After she scoffed off his argument that he didn't need to wear a helmet since he was the more experienced rider, Parker had to threaten to involve Kelly in the discussion before she hurriedly shoved the helmet on her head, giving him an evil glare in the process.

He'd deal with that versus having to explain a concussion to Kelly later.

After a few minutes of warm up on the bikes, Summer declared she was ready and pointed her bike in the direction of Newton's fields. Parker quickly threw the straps of the mostly empty backpack over his shoulders and hopped on his bike, following her out of the cul-de-sac.

The ride to Newton's Farm and Orchard was uneventful. Parker easily kept pace and used the easy ride to begin a mental list of all the questions he wanted to throw her way that day. Judging by the small grin that played on her lips, he wouldn't be surprised if she was doing the same exact thing.

Parking their bikes at the entrance of Newton's, Summer went ahead and grabbed them an empty tray to gather their berries and carefully listened to the directions of the staff, probably because she knew listening to anyone other than her wasn't one of his strong suits.

Taking the tray from her, Parker followed her lead over to one of the rows and watched as she got right to work in clearing the low plants of the fat, red, and ripe berries.

Kneeling in the dirt a few paces in front of her, Parker began to do the same. They worked in a quiet understanding for those moments, the only sound coming from either of them was the soft thumps of the strawberries being added to their tray. The quiet was fine for a while, but then Parker would look over at her lost in task and a million thoughts would flood his mind.

He thought about all the things he'd come to know about Summer, and then suddenly he'd be reminded of how little it all really amounted to.

"Hey, what's your favorite color?" His question caught her by surprise and she froze as she seemed to contemplate the question.

"My favorite color?"

"Well I already know your favorite book, so now I'm asking about which color you prefer." Parker grabbed one of the berries rubbed it on his shirt as if it'd be a suitable substitution for a sink and bit into it. The flavor exploded in his mouth as the juice dribbled down his chin. It was probably the best strawberry he'd ever tasted.

"I don't know. I don't think I have a favorite color anymore."

"Everyone has a favorite color."

"I don't know about that. That's a pretty broad claim you're making." Summer settled back onto the heels of her feet, pushing the sleeves of her shirt up to her elbows before resting her hands on her thighs for a moment. "What's your favorite color then?"

Parker thought for about half a second. "Blue."

She shook her head as if his answer tickled her. "If I had to choose a favorite, I guess I'd say my favorite would be rainbow."

Parker could have argued that rainbow wasn't a color and therefore wasn't the clear answer he was hoping for. But then he watched as she turned her face upward toward the clear blue sky, as if she hoped to see the arc of color stretched across it right then. Her smirk turned sweet and wistful. Parker decided rainbow was a perfectly acceptable answer.

"Okay. So I know your favorite book, favorite color... how about music? What's your favorite song?"

Summer shook her head, pulled out of her private revelry. "Unh-uh. I'm not telling you, you'll just laugh at me and look at me like some weirdo."

Parker's mouth gaped in offense. "When have I ever laughed at you?"

"Would you like me to list the times in chronological order or are we limiting it to the past twenty-four hours?"

She made him happy, he couldn't help but to smile and laugh when he was anywhere near her. As far as him looking at her like a weirdo, Parker was pretty sure she was getting his looks mixed up.

"I won't laugh or look at you like a weirdo. I promise." He offered her a pinky to prove his sincerity.

She pursed her lips, twisting them a bit to the side of her face as she contemplated the weight of his promise. After a heavy pause, she blew out a huff of air as she quickly locked pinkies with him.

"Antonio Vivaldi's *The Four Seasons.*"

Parker couldn't pretend he knew what she was talking about. He didn't respond as he drew his phone out of his pocket and quickly searched the song. Pressing play, the sounds of classical music filled the air around them.

While Summer's face flushed pink, Parker's face remained blank as he began to process yet another puzzling response from her. He told her he wouldn't laugh at her and he didn't want to. More than anything he wanted to laugh at himself for expecting some generic response from her. Summer had already taught him she was anything but ordinary.

"Classical, huh?"

Her eyebrows slammed together. "You promised you wouldn't laugh."

He held up his hands innocently. "I'm not laughing."

Ending the song, Parker slipped the phone back into his pocket. "Can I just say one thing?"

"What is it?"

"That song is forty-five minutes long, Summer!"

She giggled. "Maybe that's why I like it."

Parker smiled along with her. Come to think of it, maybe that's why he liked her.

Chapter Eight

Six pounds of strawberries and another task crossed off Summer's list later, Parker was back in the quiet of his bedroom. This time was a bit different. Instead of immersing himself into video games or scrolling through his Instagram and Snap Chat feeds, he collapsed onto his bed, kicking off his shoes and opening the beloved paperback she had allowed him to borrow.

After helping Summer wash her multitude of strawberries, she had decided she'd had a little too much sun that afternoon and was going to take a nap. Before Parker could get his feelings all worked up into a frenzy, she had instructed him to come back at dinner time with his books for their first attempt at tutoring. Parker dutifully agreed and headed over to his house only after a quick stop at the shed to pin their latest picture on the board and grab the book he had left behind.

In a contented quiet, Parker found a pleasant companionship in the pages of the book, connecting with the child he once was and realizing the lesson for the almost-man he was becoming.

It was a thought that occupied Parker's mind until the time on his phone's display warned him he was running late for dinner with Summer. Tossing the book down on his bed, he quickly changed his shirt before grabbing his back pack from its resting spot in the corner and hurrying out.

Summer noted his tardiness with a chastising look but coated it in forgiveness at the sight of his back pack slung over his shoulder. Her nap must have refreshed her spirit because the bossy sweetheart look was written all over her face.

He resisted the urge to pull his phone out and snap a picture of her.

Instead, he made the wise choice to collect his plate full of food and joined Kelly and Summer at the table where a glass of sweet tea sat waiting for him at what was becoming his usual seat. It felt good sitting there with them, eating dinner all together at the same time every day. It felt like he belonged. It felt like family.

Parker cleared his throat roughly. "How was your day, Kelly?"

He spied Summer biting back a smile as she speared a piece of lettuce with her fork.

"Thank you for asking! I had a surprisingly easy day, thankfully. What about you two?"

For the next thirty minutes, the conversation between the three of them flowed easily. Laughter and light teasing mixed with genuine questions of interest. It was impossible not to be around Kelly and Summer and not see the loving bond they had. He felt special to be welcomed into their lives.

Summer waved her hand in front of his face. "Yoohoo, earth to Parker! Are you done with your plate? I have dishes to wash and a game show to watch."

Parker stood and collected his dishes. "You wash, I'll dry."

The credits for Jeopardy had barely begun to roll before she was on her feet. Apparently when Summer meant they would study after the show went off, she meant down to the actual second.

"Alright, let's get to work." Summer clapped her hands giving her punctuation extra emphasis.

He groaned in mock complaint, knowing there wasn't anything short of him actually dying that was going to convince her to drop this tutoring thing.

He had already made a degree of peace with it anyway. Weighing the pros and cons against each other, he'd concluded the excuse for extra time with Summer trumped everything he had classified as a con. His coerced decision to pull his grades up had nothing to do with his parents beyond the fact that better grades would provide him with an exit strategy to graduate and get out on his own finally.

It probably had a little to do with the opinion of a certain beautiful and opinionated red-haired girl too.

She ignored his moaned protest and snapped her fingers. "On your feet, Parker Reeves, we don't have time for any slow poking about."

"Hm, slow poking huh? Maybe we should put that on our agenda for tomorrow?"

The comment was out of his mouth before he could stop it. It was bold, bolder than he intended to be with her, especially since he decided he wasn't looking for a relationship or anything.

He tempted a look at her and found Summer's face colored pink with equal parts of what he could confidently assume were embarrassment and sass. She was the only person he knew that could wear two completely different emotions on her face simultaneously.

Her lips curled up into a smile that said 'ha-ha' but her eyes told him she wasn't opposed to grabbing him by the ear (or other body parts) and setting him straight. He swallowed the bubble of nervous laughter lingering in his throat.

"I'll just grab my bag."

"Good idea." She smirked after him. "I thought we could go into the shed and study. No distractions."

Parker looked around the empty living room but shrugged in agreement. The more privacy he had the better. He didn't need Kelly, the one adult who didn't treat him like a lost cause, hearing anything about him almost blowing his chance at seeing senior year.

"Why don't you go on out there and I'll be right behind you. I'm going to grab some things from my room and then I'll meet you out there with dessert."

Dessert?

This study session thing kept getting better and better.

When Summer stepped into the shed ten minutes later with a tray that carried two dishes of strawberry shortcake, Parker felt like his eyes were about to pop out of his head.

"Did you make this yourself?"

"Yeah, well I had some help with gathering the strawberries." Settling the tray between them, she took a seat in her usual bean bag.

Parker wasn't about to wait for a written invitation to pick up a fork and try a taste. He wasn't disappointed.

Retrieving his phone, he snapped a picture of it and began posting it on Instagram. Parker had never posted a picture of anything he'd eaten on the social media platform before, but this shortcake was just that delicious.

"What are you doing?" Summer's voice came from over his shoulder.

He'd been so occupied with his post he hadn't noticed her position change. His breath caught in his throat for just a second as she sat beside him curiously checking out his phone.

He cleared his throat. "I'm posting it on Instagram. What's your handle? I'll tag you in it."

She shook her head and chortled a bit, as if it was such an insane thought. "I don't have Instagram."

"Really? What do you use your phone for then?"

"Um, to make phone calls. Sometimes I'll use it for Google and Wikipedia, but that's about it."

Parker speared another strawberry with his fork and put it in his mouth. "You're telling me you've never used social media?"

Summer shook her head, a lock of hair falling onto her face in the process. "Never really had a need for it."

"I think you'd like Instagram. You like taking pictures, it would be cool to have an account for all of them... hey, you could even start an account to post all your summer bucket list challenge pics. I bet you it'd get really popular."

She scrunched up her nose. Apparently his idea stunk. "I don't think so. The reason I like photos is because it takes something intangible like a memory and puts a piece of it right there in your hand. Besides, don't you need to have friends to make the whole purpose of social media fun?"

"I'm your friend. I'll help you set it up and everything. We can make it one more thing you've never done that you accomplish this summer."

Summer gave him a quick smile, but no answer, before crawling back to her own seat. He would drop it for now.

"This is literally the best strawberry shortcake I've ever had. How'd you learn to make it?"

"I use my phone to Google recipes too." She gave him a cheeky grin as she leaned over and grabbed the first book off the pile he'd brought along.

"Let's get to work."

And that's precisely what they did. Parker set his temperamental pride aside and listened to Summer for the next three hours. When they finally decided to call it a night, Parker happily closed his books and grabbed a water bottle from the little cooler she had set up in the corner. Their conversation from earlier worked its way back to the forefront of his mind, inciting a question he was dying to know the answer to.

"I was wondering, how come a girl like you doesn't have a bunch of friends tying up your time every day? You're nice, well at least you are to me. I guess I don't get it."

"I already told you, I got sick. People get tired of being

friends with the sick kid after a while."

Parker rubbed his hands through his hair. "Yeah, but that was such a long time ago. You're not sick anymore."

Summer offered him a tender smile that reminded him he'd never fully understand. "Once a sick kid, always a sick kid... at least to some people."

He thought about that as he collected the scratch paper they'd worked through numerous math problems on. He watched her yawn and stretch before closing the text book.

Their loss of her friendship was definitely his gain of an incredible friend.

"Thanks for doing this by the way. The truth is, I wouldn't have ever done it on my own."

"You're welcome, Parker."

Parker had stepped into his room, towel drying his hair after his shower. It had been an hour since he and Summer had parted ways for the evening with plans to meet up in the morning after breakfast. So, it was a little surprising to pick up his phone from where it lay charging to find a waiting text message from her.

Sitting on the bed, he quickly unlocked his phone. Instead of the expected witty remark or reminder of their scheduled meet time, Parker was more than pleasantly surprised to find a photo message instead. Opening it fully, his smile spread instantly at the sight of her loopy cursive written in colorful ink.

Summer had shared her list with him.

He pumped his fist in a quick celebration of victory before he lay back on his bed, looking at the list items one by one. Some were fun and silly, some more noteworthy, all of them special.

Parker: I thought your list was personal

Summer: It is. But you share personal things with friends, don't you?

Parker sat with those words for a minute, and used the time to allow himself to feel all the good feelings that surfaced with Summer's declaration of friendship. It meant more to him than he had ever expected it to.

Parker read the list no less than a dozen times before setting his phone aside for the night, eager to fall asleep so the morning would come faster.

chapter nine

Summer's face was not happy.

Parker gingerly stepped closer as he watched her frown out of the window, as if every single rain drop falling from the sky personally offended her.

"Why don't we just pick something else off the list to do?"

He pulled up the list on his phone and quickly scanned it. There were a few options he thought would sway her mood.

"What about the volunteer one? I'm sure we could find something to fulfill that one. What do you say?"

Summer shook her head a bit sadly. "I don't feel like it."

Turning her back on the window, she made her way over to sit on the couch, crossing both her arms and legs simultaneously. Summer either hated the rain or hated the fact that something other than her was dictating the plan for the day.

He looked at her and then out the window, repeating the process until he had his own lightbulb moment.

"Hey, the plan was to play in the sprinklers right? Well, let's go then."

Summer looked at him like he'd just grown a second head. "It's raining."

"I can see that. What's the difference? We were going to get wet anyway."

Summer's puzzlement gave way to a look of amusement. "You want to turn on the sprinklers in the rain? We'd look like idiots."

Parker chuckled and pulled his pouting partner in non-crime back to her feet. "We're seventeen years old about to play in sprinklers on a slip and slide, we were already going to look pretty foolish."

The sound of Summer's laughter filled the air around them as he looked down at her beaming face. Whatever had caused the cloud that shadowed her happiness that morning had finally been chased away.

He smiled at her. "Come on, what do you say?"

Summer's eyes shone with excitement. "I say I get first dibs on the slip and slide."

Parker, being the gentleman he was, allowed her to have the first and second dibs on the slide. Watching her laugh so carelessly as she ran and danced through the rain, proved without a shadow of a doubt that happiness was contagious.

Standing in the middle of a summer rain storm in her thoroughly soaked jeans and t-shirt, nothing about this girl said she was worried about anyone's opinion. And she had no need to be.

"Let's go, Parker!" She challenged him. Her eyes met her and they were alive with fun and mischief. His stomach flipped.

He had made sure to take all the necessary pictures before he returned the camera safely indoors. Tossing his shirt over the railing and leaving his shoes safe from the rain, he ran full speed across the grass before launching himself down the slippery strip of plastic. Summer's whoops of approval cheered him on as he made sure to strike his best pose at the end of his slide.

Hopping to his feet, Summer danced around him wild with excitement. "Nicely done! I give it an eight out of ten."

"An eight?! Are you blind? That was easily a nine point five!"

Summer gave a shake of her head in argument, the wet tendrils sticking to her face and neck as she did so. "Your takeoff was a bit shaky."

"I'll show you a shaky takeoff!"

With no further warning, Parker easily scooped her up, tossing her over his shoulder before running laps around the slide. Summer's yelps of protest were drowned out by the sound of her uncontrollable laughter. When Parker finally listened and put her down, they both collapsed side by side into the rain soaked grass. He closed his eyes and focused his thoughts on the rain drops falling on his face and the way his heart pounded against his rib cage when he felt Summer's hand reach over and take hold of his. Their palms pressed together, neither one of them spoke for a very long time.

The silence only broken with Summer's whispered, "Thank you."

He had a girl in his bedroom.

With the rain showing no sign of letting up any time soon, Summer had insisted on coming over to his house after she had showered and changed. She had mentioned something along the lines of just 'hanging out.' Now, Parker didn't think Summer meant the innuendo his brain heard with the suggestion, but it still didn't change the fact her presence on his bed had him feeling pretty combustible. He tried to shake it off as he watched her wander around the small space.

"It's pretty nice, though I'm not sure what kind of vibe you're going for with the whole things still in bags décor you've got going on."

Parker snorted. "That would be the 'I don't live here and I can't wait to get out of here' vibe. They've got a whole collection at Ikea now."

Summer giggled. "Ah, that explains it then. So, things haven't gotten any better with Luke then?"

"Nah." Parker leaned against the doorjamb. "To get any better we'd actually have to talk to each other and that's not going to happen, so there's that."

He could tell by the way she pursed her lips together she didn't like that answer, but she kept her protest to herself. "How long until the food gets here?"

Parker glanced at the time on his phone. "Five minutes less than the last time you asked me."

"Can't help it, I'm starved." She stopped her wandering and abruptly faced him. "Distract me."

Now Parker didn't know what the normal reaction to such a request would be, but he knew where his mind went to. He needed an activity that would allow him to pull himself together.

"We could study?" The words just felt wrong in his mouth. Next thing you know, he'd be using his phone to search random trivia and making actual voice calls.

"Eh, we can study later." She reached over and picked up one of his video games from where it lay on top of his open duffel bag. "What about this?"

"You play video games?"

"No, but you can teach me right?"

When a beautiful girl asks you to play a video game, there is only one appropriate answer. That's why they were both now sitting on the living room floor as Parker explained the ins and outs of playing Madden.

It was more than fun watching her laugh at herself as she fumbled her way through game play and then as she got into her own learning curve, watching her unleash her fiery competitive temper towards any opposing players.

Without the presence of her trusty camera, Parker had to rely on the camera of his phone to grab a shot of her. Her hair was tousled into deep waves from their water play earlier and her freckles were on perfect display. A glimpse of the tip of her tongue was caught as she ran it over her perfect pink pouty bottom lip as she intently focused on the next play.

He prepared the photo to post on his Instagram, hesitating the moment he realized once he did so, he'd be sharing her with the world. The idea unsettled him. It unsettled him the same exact way that it did every time she said his name and made him smile; the way every nerve ending in his body came alive when she touched him, even when it was simply by accident.

Parker sat back, leaning against the couch, as the full weight of realization landed on his chest. Life had just given him the mother of all plot twists.

Apparently, he (Parker Ryan Reeves) had a little bit of a crush on the girl next door.

"You going to answer the door or what?"

Her question snapped him out of his revelatory trance just in time to hear the doorbell ring again. Grabbing his wallet from the coffee table, he stumbled his way to the front door, ignoring her questioning glances.

Taking the pizza from the delivery driver, Parker pushed the whole crush on Summer thing to the back of his mind. Just because he kind of had a thing for her, didn't mean it had to change anything.

With his self temporarily reassured, he took a large bite of pizza and resumed to watching her play in between of giving her gameplay advice. When she handed the controller over to him and advised him not to blow her lead, he almost laughed aloud. But she was deathly serious, so he didn't, instead giving her an enthusiastic, "Aye-aye, Captain."

She was only mildly amused.

Playing video games with Summer, like most everything he did with Summer, felt so natural it was as if he had always done it that way. He had never met anyone ever before where they just seemed to connect so genuinely well.

"Hey, can I look at your Instagram app thingy?"

"Sure." Parker handed her his phone easily.

From time to time, Summer would ask about a picture or a person she saw as she scrolled through the recent feed. Parker hadn't bothered with it much since he and Summer had met, to be honest. He'd put up pictures but had stop bothering with checking for replies and likes.

"Are these your best friends?"

Parker paused the game, setting the controller aside before scooting over to her side to see the phone screen better.

There he was sandwiched between Kroy and Trent. The picture had been captured over Thanksgiving break when Trent's parents had taken them along to Aruba for the week.

That was just before things had gone from bad to worse for Parker.

"Yeah. Well, they used to be anyway."

"Used to? That sounds like a story." Summer set the phone down and turned to face him, propping her arm up on the couch cushion and resting her head on her fist.

"No judging?"

"I won't judge you. I promise." Her eyes were the color of sincerity, and his trust for her grew tenfold right then and there.

Parker told her all about how he'd met Trent and Kroy. He'd been the new kid in a new school and they had accepted him from day one as if he'd always been a part of their friendship. Over the next couple months, they'd grown to be inseparable, or at least that was what Parker thought.

They'd shown up for the first day of classes after the break trip to Aruba and Parker had found himself embroiled in the small Prep school's biggest scandal since... ever.

When Parker found out he was being accused of hacking into the school's closed-circuit television system and having the school's morning announcements interrupted by a rather personal (and in all honesty embarrassing) video of their Dean of Students, Parker's school career was instantly threatened with expulsion. His grades had already been taking a swift dive, and with this hanging over him, the school was ready to show him the door.

It had taken a check from his step father to change the expulsion to a suspension and keep it off his permanent record.

"But you didn't do it!" Summer's statement was seasoned with an outrage for his smeared honor. It meant more to him than he knew how to express.

"I didn't do it. But no one really asked me. Fingers were pointed at me and apparently that was all that was needed. It didn't matter what I said, so I just let them believe whatever they wanted to believe."

"But it did matter!"

"To you and me, sure. But not to them. Trent and Kroy are set to go play division I hockey next year, they couldn't risk getting expelled..."

"And you could?! What about your plans for college? Your reputation? What literal pieces of..."

"You said you wouldn't judge."

Summer rolled her eyes. "I said I wouldn't judge you,

and I'm not. I'm judging your former friends."

Parker chuckled. "Okay, then I stand corrected. It's nothing to get worked up over anymore. It's done now."

Summer simmered quietly for a moment. "I might not know a lot about having real true friends, but I know enough to know they aren't your friends, Parker."

His smile dropped from his face, looking at the carpet to distract his eyes from those soul peering ones of hers. When he looked up again, she was still there. Still watching and waiting for him to say the words he'd left unsaid since that chilly November morning last year.

"They never were."

That night Parker blocked Trent and Kroy from all his social media right before he posted the picture of Summer to his account.

@Parker_Reeves: Enjoying my Summer time.

Chapter Ten

"Remind me again why I thought it was a good idea to go outside to run around in the rain and the sprinklers?"

Summer gave him a pointed look as he joined her on the couch with his own box of tissues. When she called him that morning to cancel their plans to go hiking because she felt under the weather, Parker was bummed she didn't feel well while the relief that he wasn't the only one who felt cruddy comforted him. Still, she had insisted he come over and if they did nothing else they could at least commiserate together on the couch as they binge watched something on Netflix.

It sounded like an excellent plan to him.

Kelly had welcomed him into the house with a motherly hug. After about twenty minutes of fussing over them. She had left boxes of tissues, bottles of water and orange juice, within arm's reach as she headed off to her shift at the hospital.

"We might have gone a little bit overboard." Parker's

short chuckle sharpened the ache in his head. He dropped his head to the pillow Kelly had propped up behind him.

Summer harrumphed, pulling the crocheted throw blanket up closer to her chest. When he had arrived that morning, he'd found her in a pair of oversized sweatpants, a plain gray t-shirt, and a cardigan. Her hair was just as it was when he had bid her goodnight a handful of hours earlier, piled on top of her head. Even with her watery eyes, reddened nose, and her persistent sneezing, she was as cute as ever.

Parker was trying his best not to let this cold make him look like an utter baby in front of her. Honestly, he didn't know how well he was pulling it off.

He grabbed a tissue and gave his nose a blow. "I'm sorry. I'll make it up to you."

That piqued her interest. She reached into the pocket of her olive-green cardigan and pulled out a cough drop, "I'm listening."

"I heard there's a big Festival in town this weekend. Is it any fun?"

She gave a curious nod of her head. "The Strawberry Fest? I haven't gone every year but the times I've been able to go have always been a good time. They have people selling their crafts during the day, but on Friday night the fair opens and there's rides, games, tons of great food, and then fireworks to end it. You can see the fireworks pretty much anywhere in town that night."

"Okay. How about I take you to the fair, my treat, as an 'I'm sorry my idea got you sick'?"

Summer sneezed before a grin appeared on her face. "It's not your fault we got sick. I had a lot of fun. I just like giving you a hard time."

"Oh really? I hadn't noticed." He deadpanned. Parker nudged her feet with knee. "So... you, me, and the festival this weekend?"

Summer rubbed her lips together as she regarded him. Her head tilted to the side as her eyes fixed on his face, Parker wondered what she saw when she looked at him.

"That sounds like a pretty great Friday night."

He let out a shaky exhale. "Great. Now we precisely forty-eight hours to get ourselves healthy again."

Summer giggled as she scooted her legs over to make space for his legs to stretch out on the couch. "Well, let's get our recuperation on then!"

It was exactly what they did.

Once Summer and he had finally comprised on their Netflix binge, the two of them spent the next several hours binge watching in between their dozing and hydrating.

He looked over at where she lay on the other end of the couch and smiled. He had never had such an enjoyable time being sick as he was right then.

"Stop staring at me." Her eyes were focused on the television but her words were aimed at him. Her stuffy nose may have affected her voice but not her sass. He grinned at her.

"Can't help it. You're nice to stare at."

He hadn't meant to say the words aloud, but the sound of his own voice hit his ears at the same time as the look of curiosity came over Summer's face.

Mercifully she didn't ask any questions he didn't have the answers to right then. Instead, she threw a cough drop at his face and turned her attention back to the saga of the Dillon High Panthers football team that developed on the screen.

That evening, back in his own home, Parker sat on the bed looking at the screen of his phone, contemplating if he should finally reply to his mother's messages. He didn't quite know what to say to her at this point. She'd want to talk to him about his school work, and he wasn't ready to do that just yet. Talking with Summer about everything that went down the previous year had brought up a lot of bad feelings he had, some of which he had never even admitted to having.

Summer had known him only a fraction of the time everyone back home did, but yet and still never had to ask him if he was guilty of what he was being accused of. She knew him enough to know his character and was teeming with need to defend him. It made him think of everyone who had jumped to his worst conclusion. It made him think of his mother who had never even asked if he did it.

Before he could decide on whether he'd message her or not, his phone rung but this time it was from one of the last people he expected.

A friend from back home, though he was strongly reconsidering the whole friend label thing. He hesitated for just another moment before accepting the call.

"Parker?"

Her voice came across the line before he could even say hello.

The most popular girl in their class from one of the more popular families in their town, Kirsten had also been his girlfriend once upon a time. Their story book romance had ended before he'd even left the Dean's office, and though she insisted they have no hard feelings between them, he hadn't actually talked to her since that day.

It was good to see she still remembered his name.

"That'd be me."

Kirsten, the girl who had once captivated him, proceeded to then ramble her way through small talk about her upcoming trip to Aruba. Parker stood pacing the floor of his room hoping it'd make the conversation less painful if he could distract his brain with the activity.

Pausing by his open window, he spied the light come on in the upstairs room in Summer's house that he now knew was her room. Just the smallest acknowledgment of her presence in his life gave him reason to smile.

He cleared his throat, "I'm not trying to be rude or anything, but why are you calling me, Kirsten?"

"I suddenly have to have a reason to talk to you?"

Parker huffed out a laugh. "Uh, yeah, you kind of do. You dumped me over something so ridiculous and then you never looked back."

The line was so silent he had to make sure the call hadn't dropped.

"Who's the girl on your Instagram?"

He squeezed his eyes shut. He should have known the reason for her call. It wasn't because she missed him, or even that she cared about his well-being after his banishment to Connecticut. It was all about Summer.

His realization fizzled into humor as his shoulders began to shake with laughter.

"Are you laughing right now?"

Kirsten's upset only gave his laughing fit more encouragement. He laughed until his lungs protested with a round of coughing.

Kirsten wasn't amused. "You're so immature. I can't believe I ever dated you."

Her tone of superiority and callousness reminded him all yet another reason he felt exactly the same way about her.

It was funny how just a couple of weeks ago he might have jumped at the opportunity to talk to Kirsten again or to have any of his friends reach out to him. Now it felt like an intrusive inconvenience to his life to have to deal with any of them.

Parker ended the call because as far as he was concerned the conversation was done. He knew Kristen well enough to know she would air her grievance on her social media within the hour, so he made sure his next move was to unfriend and block her from his end. He didn't need any of her darkness creeping in and ruining his planned weekend of fun with Summer.

chapter eleven

Parker didn't see her at all on Thursday, so he was a little bit more than excited when Friday rolled around. Having beat the worst of his cold over the past two days, he woke early that morning to shower and eat breakfast before he had to tackle the task of getting dressed. Now that he'd admitted his attraction to Summer, it seemed to weigh against a lot of the decisions he made when it came to himself around her.

Decisions like should he wear a t-shirt or a polo.

Parker didn't know how much time Summer had spent getting ready but when he met her on the porch that morning he couldn't stop admiring the way the floral sundress she wore showed off her sun kissed legs. Her feet slipped into her well-worn white Converse sneakers, she made the casual outfit look stunning.

"You look great."

She let the compliment roll off of her with a chuckle. "Ready to go?"

It was a statement she had punctuated with a question mark to be polite. Summer's excitement over the Strawberry Fest and Fair the last two days had been downright contagious and Parker had stalked the clock that morning until it was time to leave.

"Well, let's get going then."

Mounting their waiting bikes, Parker once again followed Summer's lead as she pedaled the way to the Concord Fairgrounds. He was surprised to see the grounds were already buzzing with activity.

Rows of tables lined the grass where locals had displayed their goods for purchase, while a petting zoo sat ready for the little kids lined up near the pen in the other direction. Dozens of stalls were colored with bushels of fruits and vegetables ripe and ready as part of the Farmer's Market.

"Come on, Parker. They have pony rides!"

Parker fixed his mouth to protest the idea, ready to remind her he was at least three times the size of anyone the ride was actually intended for.

Summer's eyes rolled. "I just want to watch."

He had his doubts but after locking their bikes up on the designated racks, he dutifully followed her. Leaning against the railing, they both watched the mixed group of enthusiastic and reluctant riders take the reins and begin their lap.

Summer smiled brightly as she pointed out one of the little girls who happily donned a cowgirl hat over her brunette pigtails. "Look how happy she is."

Parker couldn't help but smile as he watched the little girl beam with pride as she waved to her mother as she passed.

The whole thing made Parker miss being a kid without a real care in the world. God knows that didn't last long.

The bleating of goats and more giggling children pulled his attention away from the ponies. Wordlessly, Parker moved away from Summer's side and toward the attention demanding animal. Reaching his hand over the railing he petted the friendly young goat who seemed to stare right through his skin and into his soul.

"Hey buddy..." He heard himself saying. Parker felt foolish talking to the animal right up until the second the goat responded with another bleat.

"Don't be scared little guy...or are you a girl?"

He wasn't a goat expert or anything but something about this goat felt almost kindred. He talked to the animal in quiet tones until the animal settled down. When he nudged his empty hand in request for some of the feed, Parker knew that he'd make it through the day just fine.

The sound of a camera clicking caused his head to swivel in the direction of where it came. Summer stood with her camera angled in his direction, the sound of another picture capture sounding one more time before she returned it to the small purse hung across her body.

"You going to introduce me to your friend?" She lightly teased, coming to stand by his side again.

"I would but as you can see I think I've been ditched for the lady with the food over there."

"I hate it when that happens." Summer bumped his playfully, laying her head on his arm for approximately one point two seconds.

The sweet gesture lingered on his mind for far longer.

"I want to go look at the craft tables, maybe I can find something for my mother."

"Oh, does she have a birthday coming up too?"

Summer gave him only half of a quizzical look. "No. I just feel like giving her a gift."

They leisurely walked across the grass admiring the many tables as they went. Parker stopped at a table filled with hand thrown mugs. The beautifully crafted ceramics were unique and the image of his mother using one to sip her morning coffee flashed through his mind. This had to be where his mother had gotten her beloved mug from. He wondered if either of his parents had ever brought him to this very fair when he was younger. If they had then the memory had faded under the stain of their late-night arguments and disgruntled coexistence. He shook his head gently trying to clear his mind from the remembrance.

Giving the woman a smile as he left the table behind, he spotted Summer just some ways ahead at a jewelry table. As he drew closer he watched as she slid a ring onto her finger, admiring the perfect fit. The ring was a simple thing, a skinny gold band that encased a tiny green stone.

"It's peridot." She answered his unasked question and extended her hand out in front of her giving them both a better view. "It's my birthstone."

"Pretty. It suits you."

"You think?"

He nodded, taking hold of her hand and bringing her fingers closer so he could admire how dainty and delicate the design was.

Summer slid the ring off her finger and put it back on the display rack.

"I'll just take the necklace, please." She pulled out her wallet to pay for her purchase.

"You should get the ring." Parker's voice took on a tone of insistence.

"I didn't come to shop for myself. I came for a gift for my mom and that's what I got."

She took the small box from the woman, along with her change and thanked her for her help and product, moving in the direction of the farmer's market.

Parker reluctantly stepped away from the table as well. He didn't understand girls as a general rule, but Summer was definitely one who tied his thoughts into knots.

"Mm, do you smell that?!" The change of subject wasn't lost on him, but neither was the delicious aroma filling the air.

His stomach rumbled in interest.

"Whatever that smell is I need it in my life right now."

Grabbing her hand, this time he tugged her along after him. Summer's laughter caught the breeze and trailed behind them. Food stands lined the grass offering everything from fresh baked pies and homemade strawberry jam, to grilled cheese sandwiches and funnel cakes.

Parker was in heaven.

"I've never met anyone so entirely food driven before." Summer's comment came just after Parker lamented he didn't know where to start.

"Haven't you ever heard the way to a man's heart is through his stomach?"

"Yeah, but until you I didn't really think it was a literal thing."

For the next hour Parker ate his way through most of the booths while Summer looked on in disbelief.

"You do know we're coming back tonight for the fair, you don't have to eat everything right now."

Parker's stomach begged to differ but he didn't want to waste all of Summer's time at the festival sitting at the picnic benches watching him. He pushed the almost empty cardboard tray of loaded cheese fries away from him, grabbing a napkin to wipe his mouth.

"Okay, okay, I'm done. What's the agenda for the night anyway? I know we have a list activity to tackle with winning you a prize."

"And the fireworks! We have to stay late enough to watch the fireworks."

A night of playing fair games and watching fireworks with Summer seemed like a great plan to him.

"I was thinking we could grab some Italian ice or custard for dessert to watch the fireworks with... that is if you didn't rupture your stomach already."

He patted his stomach happily. "I'll be in fine shape by then."

"What shape would that be? A circle?"

"Ha!" Parker barked a laugh at the unexpected joke, but his reply was cut short at the appearance of a new face at the table.

"Hey Summer, who's your friend?"

"Oh, hey Cara."

Cara's flaxen hair was braided back from her tan face; her baby blue eyes fixed onto Parker with the heat of an attention seeking missile.

"Parker, meet Cara. Cara, this is Parker. He's visiting Concord for the summer."

Summer stiffened as Cara made herself more comfortable on the bench next to Parker. He didn't know what the story was between the two girls but judging by how icy the atmosphere had gotten, he could wager a guess it was one of those War and Peace type stories—a long one.

Cara's hand fell on his wrist as the flirty glint in her eyes sharpened. This girl was wasting no time. "I'd love to show you around sometime, Parker. Maybe tonight?"

"I don't think so, I have plans already..." His eyes flickered over to Summer who was looking anywhere but back at him.

"With Summer? She won't mind, will you, Sum?"

He bristled at the ill-fitting nickname. Summer wasn't some... she was everything.

Parker waited for Summer to let Cara have it.

But to his surprise, she simply shrugged. "Parker can do whatever he wants to do, it's a free country after all."

She stood. "I've had bit too much sun, I think. I'm going to head back home, I'll catch you later, Parker."

Her goodbye to Cara didn't need to be spoken to be heard. She was walking in the opposite direction before Parker realized what had just happened.

He came to his feet and called after her, "Summer! Wait up!"

The words fell on the space between him and her retreating back.

Parker dropped his bike in the driveway next to hers, not stopping as he ran up the steps to her house. He rapped on the locked door, waiting only a minute before he ran around the house to the back door. The sight of her open shed door was the only thing that slowed him down. He focused on catching his breath as he neared the open door.

He knocked once before stepping through the door where he found on her bean bag writing in her notebook.

He tucked his hands into his pockets. "Hey."

Her casual "Hey" didn't satisfy him. He sat in his now usual seat.

"Why'd you run off like that?"

"I didn't run off."

Parker narrowed his eyes at her. "Why'd you walk away really fast then?"

She closed her notebook and set it aside. "Because I didn't want to be there anymore. Because I didn't want to be there while Cara was… while Cara was there."

"I take it you two don't get along."

"Maybe we did once upon a time. But then I got sick and she got mean."

Parker reached out and grabbed her hands, in one swift pull he successfully relocated her from her bean bag to his. Draping an arm over her shoulders he gave her a sideways hug.

"I wasn't going to ditch you for her. I would never ditch you, Summer, never."

They sat in the understood silence for a while, appreciating the presence of the other.

Chapter Twelve

Parker was glad Summer's spirit had been lifted in time for the evening portion of their day. After spending the afternoon lazing about her shed and talking about the sillier things in life, she had retreated into her house to take a nap. Parker had used the time alone to study, stopping just in enough time to make sure he could shower before he was due to meet her.

Dressed now in his best blue jeans, a black short sleeved button-down shirt and his sneakers, he slipped his wallet into his pocket before turning the lights off in his room.

To his complete surprise and bewilderment, Luke had arrived home about an hour ago and had brought the awkward atmosphere back with him. As he headed towards the back door, he passed where Luke stood heating a frozen dinner in the microwave.

With his hand on the door knob, Parker paused, Summer's voice murmuring in the back of his mind. "So, I'm going to the fair tonight with the girl from next door. I'll be back later."

Judging by the look of shock that claimed his face, apparently Luke hadn't anticipated being spoken to at all. "Oh, okay. Am I supposed to give you a curfew or something?"

"You could, but I'd probably break it anyway."

The two stood quiet for a moment. The hint of a smile played on Luke's usually serious face. Parker turned and pulled the door open.

"Hold up a minute, Parker. I've been thinking maybe this weekend we can clear the boxes out of your old room upstairs, that way you could have a bit more space. A boy your size can't be very comfortable in that small office..."

Parker shook his head. "The room is fine. I'll only be here until the end of summer anyway."

Parker's pointed reminder of the temporary living situation was enough to erase any trace of a smile from Luke.

Luke pulled out his wallet and extended a twenty-dollar bill towards Parker. "If you need a ride home or anything, you can call me."

Parker took the money but made no promises he didn't intend on keeping.

Parker was sitting on Summer's back porch when she emerged. She had looked beautiful earlier but in the light of the summer sunset, she was nothing short of gorgeous. Her golden red hair was curled loosely and fell around her face and shoulders like silk ribbons. She wore a black circle skirt with a dusty rose-colored tee shirt and a mini black leather backpack over her shoulders.

She held white Converse in her hands.

"You ready to go? My mom is working overnight and

she can give us a ride on her way in if we leave right now."

"Summer…"

"Yeah?"

His words were just as lost as his breath was that particular moment. "Don't forget the camera."

She spun around to show him the bag. "Already ahead of you."

He had been quiet on the ride over to the fairgrounds, something Summer had pointed out no less than five times since they'd gotten in the car.

When they'd arrived, they climbed out of the backseat, saying their goodbyes to Kelly and promising to let her know when they'd gotten back home safely. Parker took in the different scene. Gone were the craft tables that had littered the grass earlier and in their place stood dozens of carnival game booths. The sight of the colorful lights of the many rides light up the dimming sky joining the sounds of excitement filling the air.

"I think we should get my mom and Luke together for dinner."

The suggestion flew from left field and hit him smack dab in the face. "What?! Why would I ever do that to Kelly?"

Summer rolled her eyes. "My mom barely gets out of the house. She spends her time working, gardening, and pretending like she isn't watching me. She needs to start dating again."

"And you think Luke is the perfect candidate?"

"He's single, lives right next door, and believe it or not, but your dad is pretty easy on the eyes. With a little help in the wardrobe department and a reintroduction to the iron he could totally be a babe. Oh, maybe we could cook dinner for them!"

Parker shook his head furiously. The girl he was feeling did not just call his dad a babe. "Absolutely not. I like your mom too much to do that to her."

Summer pouted. "I don't think it's such a bad idea. I just thought it probably gets to be kind of lonely for Luke in that house by himself."

Parker had never thought about his dad being lonely. He had often thought about how things had gone so wrong in his family but thinking about his father coming home to an empty house and never having his family return had never come to the surface of his thoughts.

Summer walked ahead of him for a moment and when she turned back to face him, her pout had been erased with excitement.

"Let's go scope out the games." Summer gave a little skip to her step kicking up a little cloud of dust.

"A little pre-prize surveillance work, huh? I'm down. You know they stack these games to make it nearly impossible to win."

Summer had muttered some sort of acknowledgement of his warning as she slowly walked past the booths observing the current players. Parker was about to suggest they take a funnel cake break when Summer came to a stop in front of the water gun game.

"This is the one."

She paid the man her fee to play and took a seat at the only unoccupied seat. Parker stood behind her and gave her shoulders a quick massage.

"Okay, this is it. Stay loose but stay focused. Eye on the prize."

Tossing her hair over her shoulder, she gave Parker a fist bump. "Get the camera ready." It would be a lie to say Summer won the game because what she did was so much greater than the word 'win' actually felt. She'd sat in the seat for game after game, winning first place and trading up prizes until there was nothing else to upgrade to. Taking the biggest stuffed bear they had, she proudly smiled for the photo shoot Parker insisted upon. He snapped the picture for her board just before taking another with his camera. It was a picture he wanted to have with him always.

"That bear is bigger than you, Summer. We probably should have done the game last because now one of us is going to have to carry that thing around all night."

"Says who?"

And just like that, Parker watched her walk over to a young girl and her parents. After exchanging a few unheard words, Summer handed the bear over to the girl's father, waving as they happily walked away.

"You just gave away your prize!"

"Did I? Oh no, let's go steal it back from her!" She chuckled. "I said I wanted to win a prize from the fair, just to prove I could. I never said anything about keeping it."

"But if you kept it you'd be able to look at it and remember tonight."

She took the picture from his hand. "Or I could just look at the picture and remember that a few minutes later, I made a little girl's night special."

"You know something? You're pretty awesome."

"That's what all the neighbor boys tell me. Come on, Parker, let's go ride some rides."

After half a dozen rides that spun them in every sort of circle imaginable, she had decided they should slow things down a bit with a ride on the Ferris wheel. Because she was Summer, the girl who he was massively crushing on and even more, the girl who was teaching him all the things a real best friend should be. Parker sat in the bucket seat alongside her watching as the ride operator locked them in.

"Do you know why they call it a Ferris wheel?"

Parker squeezed his eyes shut as the machine lurched into motion. "Of course I don't."

"Ferris was the last name of the guy who invented it. The first one was unveiled in Chicago in 1893..."

Summer happily continued to chatter, pointing out the going-ons of things below them. Parker tried to pay attention to anything but the things below them.

"Hey, are you okay?"

Summer's hand covered his hand with its white knuckles as he applied a death grip to the safety bar.

"Parker, are you afraid of heights?"

He shook his head. "Of course I'm not. What would make you ask such a thing?"

"Oh, I don't know, maybe it's the fact that you look absolutely terrified right now!"

To her credit, Summer did not laugh at him. She didn't make any height jokes about his six-foot frame. What she did do was pry his hand from the safety bar and interlace their fingers together.

He licked his lips nervously. "I'm not afraid of being up high. It's the falling thing that gets to me."

From his peripheral he could see her nod. "I get that. Care if I make a suggestion?"

"Sure." Anything to distract him from the descent about to happen in a second.

"Instead of looking down. Look up." She used her free hand to tip his chin upwards. "Look at that Parker."

Now that the sun had took its final dip below the horizon line, hundreds of twinkling stars had already come out to shine in the dusky purple sky. The tightness in his chest eased and Parker took his first real breath in minutes.

"It's beautiful, isn't it? It's hard to think about anything bad when you're looking at something so beautiful."

Parker turned to face her, their eyes meeting and holding each other's gaze. His heart calmed entirely and allowed his body to relax. "You're beautiful."

Blushing she bit her lip and started to shake her head.

"You are."

His eyes jumped between her eyes and her lips as she spoke her quiet thanks.

The ride had paused, keeping them on the top for a long moment.

"Need to look up again?"

He shook his head, keeping his eyes locked onto hers. "Nope. This is perfect."

Her cheeks still flushed with the compliment. She

tucked her hair behind her ear. "Take a picture with me Parker."

Once off the ride, Parker convinced Summer to go and find them a spot to watch the fireworks from while he went to find needed sustenance. When he rejoined her loaded up with a tray full of a powdered sugar covered funnel cake and an extra-large frozen vanilla custard buried with rainbow sprinkles, Summer gave him a look of disbelief.

"I still don't know how you do it."

"And by it you mean..."

"Eat all that stuff and still manage to look like you stepped off a Hollister ad."

Summer had yet to say anything that gave him any sort of indication she found him attractive so he was taking this one to the bank.

Parker ripped off a piece of the funnel cake and put it in his mouth. The warm dough causing him to smile even brighter. "I have a high metabolism. Besides, I got this for us to share."

He eyed her eagerly take the plastic spoon and dig into the frozen dessert just as the front sky lit up pink and purple with the first boom of the fireworks.

There was something about watching fireworks that always made him happy. But watching Summer watch fireworks? That was a whole other and newly incredible feeling. Her face had captured his interest so wholly that he'd witnessed just about the entire show by the reflection of colors in her irises.

He'd been worried that after he finally found the friend

he'd so desperately needed, he'd lose her with the romantic complications that would undoubtedly follow once he confessed his feelings. But it wasn't until then he realized if he took it serious, if he treated it as real, maybe one thing didn't have to cancel out the other.

He watched as she lay propped up on her elbows, her face tilted heavenward. Her perfect pink lips parted in subtle awe, the corners tipped upwards in a persistent smile.

"Summer?"

She pulled her eyes away from the sky, turning her face toward him. "Yeah, Parker?

Without waiting for his doubt to talk him out of it, he closed the gap between them, pressing a gentle kiss to her lips.

And then another.

His hand cupping her jaw gently before burying itself into her silky curls and supporting the back her neck as she kissed him back, deepening their kiss and his feelings for her with every second it consumed.

Parker's tongue found hers at the sound of the start of the firework finale.

Summer tasted like soft vanilla ice cream drizzled with rainbow sprinkles. She tasted like dancing in the rain and riding bikes in the sunshine. Like pop rocks and soda pop, his head and his heart was going to explode.

The walk home was quieter than Parker would have liked. After what had been the best kiss of his life, Parker was left hoping he hadn't just ruined the best friendship of his life.

Summer's chatter had diminished to one-word replies and nods of her head in response to any of the questions he threw her way in hopes he'd get some sort of real response out of her.

Back in their cul-de-sac, they reached Parker's driveway first. Parker took her hand in his and gave it a small squeeze.

"Should I be apologizing right now?"

Summer shook her head. "There's nothing to apologize for Parker. I had a good time."

"So, I'll see you tomorrow then?"

He hated that he had to ask. The insecurity overtaking the confidence he'd had when he kissed her just an hour ago.

"I'll be over after breakfast."

"K. Text me when you're in the house and lock it up after yourself for the night."

She nodded, stepping away from him and letting her hand fall back to the side. Parker watched as she walked into her house. As she closed the door behind her, he couldn't help but notice that she hadn't looked back at him once.

Chapter Thirteen

Parker tapped his pen against the still blank page of his notebook. Summer was late. It wouldn't be a big deal if it had been anyone else, but it wasn't. This was Summer, the girl who felt like if you weren't ten minutes early to something, you were late. Parker picked up his phone and contemplated texting her again, the only thing stopping him was the memory of their kiss the night before and how quiet she was afterward.

His stomach churned with an awful feeling of fear and regret; his fear and her regret. Parker picked up his pen and resumed his notebook tapping. He'd wait another five minutes, then he'd call her.

Two and a half minutes later, Parker watched Summer cross the yard to the patio table where he sat waiting. The oversized long sleeve black tee shirt dwarfed her small frame, the bottoms of her cut off jean shorts only peeking out as she walked toward him barefoot.

"Sorry I'm late, I overslept."

Parker stifled his panicked feelings enough to muster up an amused grin. "Whoa, I was up before you? The student is becoming the master."

"Easy, let's not get ahead of ourselves."

Her tone was friendly enough but Parker wanted to see the solemn expression on her face change.

For the first time since he'd met her, things between them felt forced, the tension troubling the usual easy flowing current of their relationship. The idea of working through pages of boring equations suddenly seemed even duller.

"Did you eat yet? I can whip up a mean Toaster Strudel."

"I'd rather get straight to work if you don't mind, I have some stuff I need to do later."

Summer's rejection of his breakfast offer didn't surprise him. It was the 'stuff' thing that had him stuck in his feelings. Summer said she had stuff to do, but he had heard what she meant, the stuff didn't include spending any more time than necessary with him. It stung.

Pushing his book away from him, he angled himself toward her. "Should we just talk about it?"

Summer wrapped a strand of hair around her finger, shrugging a shoulder in his direction. Her eyes stayed focused on his math book.

"Summer, will you at least look at me for a second?"

She obliged but only for a literal second. "So, if you can get through this section with no problem, I think we can power through to the next unit. I looked up some SAT testing dates and there's a few that might work for you at the end of the summer."

"God, Summer, I don't want to talk about SATs or differential equations. I want to talk about you and me. I want to talk about how last night I kissed you and how it was the best kiss ever, complete with fireworks and I'm not talking about the literal ones."

She sighed and squeezed her eyes shut. "I can't do this with you, Parker."

"You kissed me back, Summer."

"I know I did, and it was a mistake. You're here for what another seven weeks? Then you're going back to your life in New York and I need to deal with my own life here. That kiss shouldn't have happened."

Her chair scraped along the wooden patio as she pushed herself back on to her feet and began her retreat. Parker caught up with her before she could reach the fence.

"Don't do that. Don't call it a mistake. I'm an expert at mistakes, I spent the last year making one after another. Last night... kissing you... that was perfection."

"Parker- "

He held up a hand, halting her words, needing to get the words out of his heart before her words broke him. "You're my best friend. You're my best friend and you're the girl I can't stop thinking about. And I don't want to stop. So, I can't apologize for kissing you, because if you could see how much I feel for you then you would know that kissing you is just one thing on the list of things I want to do with you."

Her eyes met his, watery with emotion. "This is insane."

He shook his head, taking her hands in his own. "These few months, they don't have to be it for us. I can come back and visit on breaks until graduation. I'll get my act together and we can apply to colleges…"

"Parker, stop! Don't be stupid. You can't build your future plans around me. It was one kiss that I shouldn't have let happen. I knew better."

"It's not only about the kiss!"

She pulled away from him and took a step back. The distance between them feeling more insurmountable with every second that passed.

Parker looked at her, the girl who'd captured his interest from the very first second he laid eyes on her. Her eyes that were always lit up with passion for even the most mundane things had been extinguished. Everything he loved most about her had been suddenly shuttered.

"What about the list?"

It wasn't the question he intended to ask but it hung there between them with the heavy weight of all the important unasked ones.

"I'm done with the stupid list, Parker." She hopped the fence before running across her yard and back into her house, undoubtedly locking the door behind herself.

It had been exactly forty-eight hours since Parker had seen or talked to Summer. After their regrettable parting at the fence, Parker wallowed in his own feelings for a few hours, wondering how the day would have played out if he had just allowed her to pretend like Calculus was the most important thing they needed to discuss. After he'd had enough of feeling sorry for himself, he'd picked up the phone and called her, only to be sent straight to voicemail. That was how it went with every call; his text messages sent without reply.

With no desire to play video games or pretend to have anything to say to anyone back home, Parker missed her more than he imagined he would.

With nothing better to do, he'd spent most of the last two days studying and reviewing all the notes Summer had written up for him. When the third morning came with no waiting messages from her, the last thing he wanted to do was deal with a pile of school texts.

After he and Luke semi-awkwardly maneuvered around each other in the kitchen over breakfast, Parker found himself in the garage pulling out the lawn mower he'd seen stashed in the corner. Dusty from a lack of use, Parker figured Luke had taken to paying some neighborhood kid to take care of it. Checking that it indeed had fuel, he went to work. Mowing the front and back lawn of his father's house, had been physical enough to distract him from the idea of banging down Summer's door for a couple hours in the morning but all his feelings bubbled back to the surface the instant he'd caught a glimpse of her as she and Kelly left the house and slipped into the car. Kelly waved at him as she drove past him, Summer did not. He pulled off his shirt, used it to wipe his brow free of sweat and then tucked it into the waistband of his shorts before he pushed the mower over to their front lawn and went back to work.

That evening, he pretended to be asleep when he heard Luke talking to Kelly at the front door. She'd come over with batch of chocolate chip cookies to thank him for mowing her yard. But she wasn't the neighbor he wanted to talk to, so he ignored his father's knocking on the door. He lay still until real sleep overcame him and his thoughts of her became dreams.

On his fourth Summer-less day, Parker got on his bike and found his way to the center of town. Thanks to a quick search on his phone, he located a suitable barbershop where he got himself a long overdue haircut and directions to the library. Following the easy instructions, he wandered and walked along the sidewalks and admired everything from the small shops that lined the street to the potted plants around the base of the street lamps. All of it added another layer of quaint charm to the town.

There was something about Concord that made it easy to see why people seemed to enjoy living there as much as they did. Now that he had his attitude in check, it didn't feel quite as stifling as it had weeks ago.

But to its benefit, Concord also had Summer, and anything Summer touched seemed to radiate with light, love, and happiness.

He missed her.

Parker climbed the wide set stone steps to the front door of the library. Pulling one of the heavy doors open, he was suddenly hit with a whoosh of cold air and the scent of books. A few weeks ago, the library was probably one of the last places you would have been able to find him. But after reading the book he borrowed from Summer about five times that week, he decided he should see about getting himself some more age appropriate reading material.

With the rows of bookshelves that awaited him, there was only one problem, Parker didn't know where to begin. He scanned the room for the librarian with the nicest smile. Finding her, he cleared his throat and did the one thing that had always been a little bit hard for Parker to do, he asked for help.

Thanks to one of the sweetest librarians he was sure to have existed, later that afternoon Parker sat on the front porch with a new book in hand. He read until the light of the sun began to dwindle, surprising himself when he realized he'd lost himself in the words for such a stretch of time.

Closing the book, he stood and stretched his back, his eyes automatically drawn to Summer's closed door. After days of waiting for her to open it, Parker found himself moving in its direction. He rapped it knuckles against the smooth wood before stepping away to grab firmly onto his mixed emotions.

And then she was in front of him once again. Her soft ember colored hair loosed and wild, falling in waves around her face. The large loose knit sweater she wore bared one of her shoulders and fell halfway down her petite frame.

"Parker..."

"This is getting ridiculous. I want us to talk."

She pressed her lips together for just a second. She looked at him, long enough for him to see the storm clouds brewing in her eyes. "It's not a good time."

"It's been days."

"I know-"

"Summer, did I leave my keys down there?" Kelly's voice rang out and interrupted her words. It was the break in conversation that allowed Parker to focus on something other than Summer's face for a moment. The suitcase that stood waiting by the door in particular.

His heart thumped hard in his chest. "You're leaving?"

Summer's face stayed solemn as she gave him one

affirmative shake of her head. "For a couple of days. We'll be back on Sunday."

"Maybe Sunday night would be a good time for us to have a chat then?"

The maybe she left him with as he watched her get into her mother's car and promptly place ear buds into her ears gave him his first bit of hope that his Summer time wasn't quite over just yet.

Summer: Meet at shed after Jeopardy.

Parker had read and reread the simple message from Summer. The last couple of days in her absence had been filled with new questions and deeper emotions. He'd wondered where she had gone, but felt an overwhelming relief that she'd come back.

chapter Fourteen

For the first time in a week, Parker slipped the key into the lock and opened the shed. Nothing was noticeably different. No new pictures had been pinned to the board. No new books lined her shelves. Everything had been left exactly as it was, and yet everything had changed.

Parker stood with his hands into his pockets as he waited for the door to swing open for her. It was seven thirty-two when he heard the knob turn.

Summer stepped into the space and Parker felt his lungs let go of all the air they were holding hostage.

She was here.

The hard part was going to be put behind them.

He was going to get his Summer back.

Her hair had been swept up into a neat bun, her hands tucked into the pocket of her zipped hoodie. She shifted from one pink Converse covered foot to the other, momentarily pulling his attention from her face to those legs of hers.

"Hey, Parker."

Her voice soothed him in a way he didn't know a voice could. He smiled just a bit.

"Hey, Summer."

She scanned the room much as he did. Parker wondered if she was also thinking about how much had changed between them in the week.

Summer sat on the floor crossing her legs. "Will you sit with me?"

Parker couldn't think of a single thing he wouldn't do for her, so of course he sat. "Where'd you go, Summer?"

"I had to go up to Boston-"

Parker shook his head. "That's not what I meant. I mean where did you go? After the night at the fair, you checked out. At first, I thought it was because of me, but I had some unexpected alone time to think and realize not everything is about me. Am I right?"

Summer's mouth opened and closed. Seeing her at a loss for words wasn't a familiar sight for him. Then instead of speaking, she blew out a breath and brought a shaky hand to the zipper pull of her sweatshirt. Parker watched in near disbelief as she slowly and steadily eased the zipper down. Parker's mouth went instantly dry and his heart raced, unaware of what was happening or why it was, but in fervent approval. She sat in front of him in her soft gray cotton bra, baring not just her skin, but her secret.

She gently touched the scar that ran down the center of her chest, in the sweetest valley he had ever seen.

"I was born with a heart defect. My parents didn't know

anything was wrong until one day in kindergarten I passed out. I spent months in the hospital, being open and closed until I was stable enough to go home. I've had three more surgeries since then."

Parker's hand found hers and clasped on tightly. He had known she'd been sick as a child from the first day they met. However she never talked about it any further, and he'd been too distracted to ask. His eyes moved from her scar back to her face as she cleared her throat before continuing.

"Remember the night we rode the Ferris wheel, how we talked about fears? Well here's the thing, heights, drowning, giant poisonous spiders, none of that ever scared me. I've already been through some of the worst." She looked down at her own chest, a small smile of derision danced on her lips. "When I was six years old, the doctors told my mom I wouldn't make it to see seven. I made my peace with life and death that day, just like I've done with every day since. I know my odds and I play the hand life dealt me. But then you came along, Parker. You showed up next door, became a friend, my only and my best. And then you started to feel like so much more. After we kissed that night, I did get mad, but it was at myself. Spending time with you had made me forget all about my reality, and for the first time in years I felt resentful and afraid. Before you I had a plan to make no plans but now… I want more."

The impact of her words hit him squarely in the chest, each syllable heavier than the last. He wanted to make it all better, to find the right words to say that would be enough to ease the lines of worry that took up the space where her smile should be.

Parker came to his knees in front of her, gently cupping

her face with his hands. "I told you once and I'll tell you again, I'm not going anywhere. Neither are you for that matter. We're in this together now, and if I have to spend the rest of the summer proving it to you, then I will."

He wiped the wetness from her cheeks with the pads of his thumbs tracing the freckles that he loved so much. His heart swelled with affection. The seriousness of everything she just told him coursed through his veins but it didn't dilute the sincerity of his words.

"Parker-"

He kissed away whatever sensible argument she was going to offer. Her lips immediately yielded and responded to his. She tasted just as sweet as he remembered.

"Also, feel free to never wear a shirt again when we're alone."

Her laughter filled the room and instantly brought a smile to his face. Side by side they lay facing each other, her lips just a breath away from his. "I missed you, Summer. You're beautiful and sexy, bossy and fun, and I missed you so freaking much."

"You're so cute it's ridiculous, you're an amazing kisser, you eat more than anyone I've ever known, and I missed you even more."

Parker grinned, placing his hand above the waistband of her leggings and pulling her closer. The warmth of her skin radiated through the thin cotton of his shirt. He felt her steady heart beat and couldn't believe there could ever be anything wrong just below the surface.

Tomorrow they could talk more about everything, he would ask her questions and insist on learning anything he needed to know, but tonight he just wanted to hold her close and pretend the rest of the world didn't exist.

Parker didn't know how to feel the next morning. The girl he'd spent his summer with thus far had always been in his mind such a formidable force of nature. Last night, she had shown him such a vulnerable layer of herself, and true to Summer's uncanny ability to make everything she touched shine as if dipped in pure sunlight, her vulnerability was even more beautiful than she was.

He looked over at her as she lay beside him as the merry go round spun them in slow lazy circles. She looked fragile. Not in the sense that she was weak, Summer was anything but. She was fragile in the way one of those fancy artifacts they kept behind glass at museums. The kind that were intricately beautiful because they had survived the rough passage of time and had become even more valuable because of it.

"Are you staring at me, Parker Reeves?"

Her eyes were closed but her telling smile told him that he was busted. He grinned. "Maybe."

He shuffled his feet giving the apparatus just a bit of energy to set them off moving again. Pointing to the sky he nudged her.

"Look that one looks like an ice cream cone."

"How come every cloud you see resembles some type of food?" Summer propped herself up on her elbow.

"Maybe it's because I'm starving."

Summer rolled her eyes with affection. "Your brain is in your stomach."

He wasn't so sure about that as his eyes dipped to the

low neckline of the tank top she wore that day. Her change in wardrobe had been a very pleasant surprise.

"You lured me out of the house with the promise of ice cream!"

She laughed and sat up fully. Dropping her feet to the woodchips below, she brought them to a stop. Despite his protests for food, Parker was in no hurry to move.

"I was thinking about what thing we should cross off the list next."

"You still want to help me with the list?"

Parker sat up in confusion. "Why wouldn't I?"

She caught her bottom lip in between her teeth for a second, her cheeks flushing pink. "To be honest, I thought you were only helping me as a way to… I don't know… get my attention or something."

"And now that I have your attention, you think I'd forget all about it?"

She nodded, tucking her hair behind her ear. "I mean, it's kind of silly."

"But it's not, though. Your list is the reason why this is going to be probably the most productive summer I've ever had." He pressed a soft kiss to her cheek. "You're not a quitter Summer, I can't let you quit on this list either."

"Okay then. What are you thinking?"

Parker hopped to his feet pulling her along with him. "I can explain better over ice cream."

After a few searches of the internet and a phone call, Parker had planned out the afternoon's activity. Hopping back onto their bikes, Parker followed the guiding voice of his phone's navigation system with Summer riding right alongside of him.

Coming to a stop in front of the squat brick building surrounded by lush green grass and indoor and outdoor kennels, Summer grinned.

"We're volunteering?!"

Her enthusiasm would have been contagious if his own excitement hadn't been at peak levels already. After a tough week, Parker couldn't think of anything better than an afternoon spent playing with animals.

He set their bikes securely into the bike rack before pulling the door open for him to enter the cheerful space. Mary Ellen, the shelter director, had been waiting to greet them and stepped forward.

"Hi, you must be Parker! We spoke on the phone this morning. I'm so glad you could make it in."

Mary Ellen had a kind face that matched her voice. He shook her hand. "Thank you for having us. This is Summer. We'd be happy to help with anything around here today."

Mary Ellen smiled even brighter as she shook Summer's hand as well. "How about a quick tour and then we'll get to putting you young ones to work."

Two hours later, Parker had finished cleaning out all the kennels before refilling food and water bowls, smiling at Summer every time they crossed paths. Following the sound of unabashed laughter, Parker stepped out into the outdoor area and was greeted by the sight of Summer laying in the grass playing with a few scampering pups. He pulled his cell phone out of his pocket, quickly capturing a few pics of the moment. Nothing could ever sound as perfect as the sound of Summer's laughter ringing out clear and pure on such a picturesque summer day.

"Room for one more at this party?"

He took a seat at her side, stretching his legs out parallel to hers. One of the puppies promptly scurried onto his lap. Parker gave the pup an affectionate round of petting as Summer looked on. "He likes you. You should adopt him."

He cocked an eyebrow in her direction. "Luke doesn't want me around, I doubt he'd agree to a four-legged house guest joining us."

"Is he really that bad? Luke, I mean. I was kind of hoping things would start to get better between you two."

He shrugged both shoulders. "Maybe it is. We talked in actual complete sentences last time."

"Maybe he'd open up more after dinner..."

Parker shook his head. "If you're about to say what I think you're about to say, please don't say it."

Summer turned to face him, resting on her knees. "You said you would think about it."

"And every time I think about setting up my girl's mother with my estranged father, I'll be honest, it kind of makes me want to throw up."

The corner of her lips turned upwards. "You just called me your girl."

"Did I?"

"You definitely did." Setting the puppy aside, she threw a leg over his lap and straddled him. "And I kind of liked it."

"So maybe I should call you 'my girl' more often then."

She nodded. "I'm about to kiss you, Parker Reeves."

"Right here? In front of the puppies?!" He feigned shock and modesty.

Summer tossed her head back in laughter right before she brought her lips to his and kissed him tenderly, and then not so tenderly when her bossy little tongue demanded more.

"Today was a good day."

The two of them sat on Summer's back patio and sipped some of the sweet tea Summer had brought out for them. He couldn't have agreed with her any more than he did.

"You know volunteering looks really good on a college application."

Parker gave her a sideways glance. "I should have known somewhere in that brain of yours, you'd be concocting a plan to save me from a life of leisure."

Summer's smirk told him he was right. "Mary Ellen said we'd be welcome back at any time."

"Well that's good to know. I was hoping she didn't bar us for life after that kiss you laid on me."

Even though it was just the two of them in a private moment, Summer blushed because that was the type of girl she was. She was the type of girl that had him wanting more than he had ever wanted before.

This girl was a girl who didn't just give him something pretty to look at. She gave him a purpose. It was everything about the way she looked at him that made him want to be the guy that she seemed to see. If he knew nothing else, Parker knew this: he would be that guy and he would keep her heart.

Chapter Fifteen

Parker didn't think Summer could make him want to look at her any more than he already did. And then she put on a bikini.

He would have liked to think when he agreed to a beach day, it was because of the ulterior motive of seeing her in as little as possible. But in truth, it was hot and humid and there was nothing to do but dump yourself in water or hide somewhere that had central air conditioning.

"You look... amazing."

The word didn't feel like it was enough but yet it was the only word that seemed to fit how incredible she looked. The color splashed fabric made her hair seem more vibrant and the exposure of her ivory skin revealed more splashes of those cinnamon freckles. She immediately placed a subconscious hand over the vertical scar on her chest. Insecurity colored her face in a way that agitated his heart.

He dropped his towel to the sand along with their bags

and closed the gap between them. Running his hands up and down the smooth skin of her arms he locked eyes with her, their connection transcending physical touch. Gently he covered her hand with his own, feeling her heart beat for just a moment before he removed both of their hands from her chest and revealed her line of courage once more. He kissed it. Once. Twice. Three times.

"You look absolutely amazing."

Somewhere underneath their kiss he tasted the words of thanks on her tongue. He felt her self-confidence as she wrapped her arms around his waist and sighed into him.

Right in the middle of that kiss was Parker's most favorite place.

They had splashed and swam, lazily floating on the salty waves and kissing as if they had invented it. As they lay on their towels exhausted from hours of romping through the surf and sand. Summer's question caught him by surprise.

"What do you want to be when you grow up?"

"Do you want the real answer? Or the one for the guidance counselors and demanding parents?"

Summer rolled to her side facing him. Her wet tendrils of hair coated in sand, her cheeks pink from the heat. "Real. I always want real from you."

"I just want to be happy." He ran a hand over the back of his neck hoping that his answer didn't scream 'complete lame loser.' It was his truth.

Summer reached out and gave his hand a squeeze. "I think happy is always a good goal."

"You know for the first time in a long time I actually have a few of those."

"Goals?"

Parker nodded. "For a long time, I felt like I was stuck doing the things I had to do, but now I actually have some things I want to do."

She tapped a finger to her chin, drawing his attention from her playful eyes to the perfect pout of her lips. "Tell me more, Parker Reeves."

"I want to travel. Not on some fancy yacht or in fancy hotels like my stepdad though, I want to pack a back pack, buy an open-ended ticket and just experience it."

"That sounds pretty thrilling."

"What about you? What's something you want to do?"

"I don't know. I've never really thought about it. This whole list deal is the closest thing to making plans I've ever done. It's hard to make plans when your health always seems to interfere."

Parker swallowed the reminder of Summer's reality thus far. He handed her the perfect seashell he'd been handling.

"Close your eyes."

He waited until she did before continuing. "Imagine you could go anywhere right now. Somewhere you'd be happy to spend your days. Now tell me, where are you?"

He watched her face closely. Studying the way the tip of her tongue ran across her bottom lip, almost as if she wanted to taste the words before she spoke them. Memorizing the way her eyelids fluttered just before she opened them again.

"With you."

Two simple words had never meant quite so much to him. Being real with her had opened his eyes to the truth, and the truth was his problems never seemed to matter as much whenever he was with this girl. His life never seemed as bright as it did now that he knew her. He never wanted to let that feeling go.

"I want to make you happy, Summer. I want that more than anything."

Cupping his jaw in her hand she smiled. "You do. I am."

He was too. More than ever before, he was happy.

"Take a picture with me."

"They have two weekends at the end of August open for SAT testing not too far from here."

Parker pushed the pin through the top of the Polaroid mounting it securely to the corkboard. He smiled at the captured image of Summer posing with the massive sand castle they spent the afternoon constructing with the help of several eager children.

"Are you even listening to me, Parker?"

"I was until I heard the word test." He tossed her a cheeky grin to which she rolled her eyes. "I agreed to let you help me catch up on school work and get through this summer's worth of work. I don't recall ever mentioning anything about SATs."

"You're going to have to take them anyway. You should take them at least twice. School admission will take the better of the scores with your application."

Tests, college admissions, his head was beginning to swim with other people's expectations of him. "I don't even know what I want to do with my life. I might not even want to go to college."

"But you might and if you do, you're going to need to

take the SATs, so let's just get it out of the way right?"

Parker sat in the bean bag chair and let his head roll backward. Summer's logic made sense as it always did.

"I just don't know why I should put so much effort into something everyone else already thinks I'm going to fail at."

Summer closed her laptop and set it aside. Her frown had overtaken her entire face.

"I don't think you're going to fail. As a matter of fact, I know you're not going to fail."

Her vote of confidence in him made his heart constrict with emotion. It had been a long time since he'd felt someone back him up and go to bat for him as much as Summer did. She had this special way of looking at him and seeing someone no one else bothered to look for. She saw him.

"You're smart, Parker. You have a good heart, and because of it you are going to do great things for the world."

He pulled her into the space next to him where she fit perfectly under his arm. The missing puzzle piece in his life completely filled by her presence. For weeks he wondered what he would say to his mother when he could no longer avoid conversation with her. With the girl next door in his arms giving him all sorts of reasons to make plans, Parker could only think about saying thank you.

"Email me those testing dates later."

chapter sixteen

He drummed his fingers against the smooth top of the desk where he sat at the back of his father's classroom. Waking up that morning, he didn't know that a few hours later he'd be sitting here. He pulled his baseball cap down lower on his head, unsure if he wanted to reveal his presence just yet.

His phone buzzed in his pocket and without looking at the screen he already knew who it was. He'd left the house early that morning without telling Summer of his plan to audit his dad's class. If he had told her, she would have volunteered to come along with him for moral support, and he would have jumped at the offer. But he knew this was something he needed to do on his own. After spending all night thinking about her vote of confidence in his future and how far she'd help him come thus far, Parker knew it was time for him to deal with some things, two of them being his father and his plans for college.

So, here he sat.

Bodies slowly filed into the room around him, quiet

chatter drowning out the second thoughts he was having. Parker shifted in his seat hoping he blended in enough to avoid any questions about his sudden attendance. A minute before the class was set to start, Luke entered the room. He wore the same thing Parker had watched him leave the house in. His hounds tooth blazer lay draped over his arm, his light gray dress shirt still remained properly buttoned and his perfectly tied bow tie sat just so. The girl next to Parker audibly sighed as Luke pulled his glasses out of his pocket and slid them on. Summer's voice piped up somewhere in the back of his head telling him his father was pretty easy on the eyes.

Parker shuddered at the thought and tried to shake it away. Still, just imagining Summer's voice caused a smile to spread across his face that wasn't so easily shook.

"Good morning..." Luke's words faltered and he cleared his throat. His eyes met with Parker's then. A mixture of shock and surprise coloring his normally hazel irises. Parker swallowed, keeping his face stoic, not wanting to betray his feelings.

To Luke's credit, he did a decent job of erasing the emotion from his face and going on to teach a surprisingly entertaining and educational class.

Parker had never imagined his father to be as charismatic as he was as he strolled throughout the room. The rapport he had with his students was evidence today hadn't been a fluke, or better yet a show on his behalf. As the class began to file out, Parker was left with a whole new set of questions and a burning curiosity about the father he barely knew.

"Parker." Luke stepped forward just as the door closed behind the last exiting student.

"I have to give it to you Luke, you are a much better professor than you are a father."

The light-hearted confidence Parker had seen Luke exhibit for the last seventy-five minutes now diminished right before his eyes. For the first time since Parker had been back in Concord, he realized it was uncertainty rather than apathy that kept Luke skirting around conversation.

Parker stood, coming eye to eye with him. "You invited me to come audit your class, I decided to take you up on it."

"I'm glad you did." Luke gave him an almost apologetic smile before taking his glasses off, using two fingers to squeeze the bridge of his nose. "Parker, I, uh, well the thing is- do you think maybe you'd like to go grab some lunch? I have some time before my next class. Maybe we could talk?"

Saying no to Luke was practically a natural reflex at this point and he was shaking his head before Luke could even finish his invitation.

"Parker, please-"

He didn't know which was worse, the idea of talking about a future in college with his father or talking about the past with his father. Both topics had him wishing he could teleport himself anywhere else. No, not anywhere else, just to a certain red-haired girl's shed.

"I have to go. I need to swing by the admissions office and pick up some information before I head back to meet Summer." Parker cringed as the confession rolled off his tongue with ease. He rubbed his palm into his forehead.

"Let's not make this into some big thing, alright? I just want some information to look over. I don't need you running and telling my mom about any of this. God knows, her favorite hobby is making things into big deals when it comes to my life."

Luke nodded, his smile a little bit more understanding this time. "Of course. Well, I'll let you get on with the rest of your day. But if you need some help with your decision or if you just want to talk..."

Parker gave a short nod of his head and gestured around the room. "I know where to find you."

Ignoring the flash of distress that crossed his father's face at the dig, he forced his lips into a thin smile as he walked around the desk and headed to the exit at the back of the classroom. With his hand on the doorknob, Parker paused, his conscience once again sounding a lot like Summer. Drawing in a breath, he turned around. "If you think you can manage to be home on time for dinner tonight, maybe I could make sure that I'd be in the mood for some Chinese take-out."

Luke's smile spread then. He'd forgotten what his father's smile looked like until that very moment. Parker dipped his head and pushed his way through the door.

Summer placed the brochure back on the floor between them. They sat on the floor of her living room, the muted television flickering as she listened to the story of his morning. Her eyes were brimming with happiness as she grinned.

"Oh Parker, I'm so proud of you."

"Even if I do apply, it's just an application." He tried to shake off the praise with nonchalance.

Summer wouldn't be stopped, though. "I'm not talking

about the application. I'm talking about you. You did something tough today and took a huge step forward."

"I think huge is a bit of an overstatement."

Summer playfully kicked at him with her bare foot. "Will you shut up and let me be proud of you?"

"Ugh, I guess if you insist."

Parker lifted his arm and welcomed her as she curled into his side. With so many of his feelings coming to the surface today, Parker relished the one he was feeling right now.

"You're going to do so much good, Parker Reeves. I can feel it in my bones."

"You make me want to be one of the good ones."

She shook her head against him, the movement filling his nostrils with a fresh whiff of her shampoo. She smelled like heaven. "You're already one of the good ones."

Parker's chest shook with a stifled chuckle. "You make me want to be better than good then."

He kissed her forehead softly. Then, just as he expected, she tilted her head backward, offering up her lips to him. It was a gift he hastily took. It only took a one second taste of Summer for him to completely lose himself in her.

"Best. Ever." Two words now lost in the middle of a kiss that Parker was certain he would remember for the rest of his life.

Nothing could compare to the way she felt under his hands. Her petal soft skin warmed his palms as he pulled her close, her fingers pressing into the planes of muscle just beneath the thin cotton of his t-shirt.

"Ahem."

The sound of Kelly clearing her throat from the entry way was probably the only thing that could have gotten him to pull away from her. He immediately released his hold on her and tried his best to look completely innocent. The idea of Kelly now banning him from her home and his daughter sent his mood spiraling downward. Summer on the other hand didn't seemed as bothered as she flashed a smile at him. "Oops."

"Well, this is new." Kelly's voice was lighter than Parker had expected it to be though tempered with caution. Parker didn't know how it would feel to walk in on your teenage daughter getting pretty thoroughly kissed by the boy next door, but it was safe to say that Kelly was taking things far better than he could have ever predicted.

"So this," She waved her fingers at the two of them. "This is a thing now?"

"Yes ma'am." Parker nodded as Summer slipped her fingers between his. The physical connection instantly anchoring him in the moment.

"I can honestly say I'm surprised... it's taken this long." Kelly flashed them both a smile. "Do I have to give you both the talk now?"

Summer physically recoiled. "One time was enough for a lifetime."

Turning to Parker she rolled her eyes. "You haven't lived until you get the talk from your mother, the nurse. She actually uses props and pictures to make it fun."

Everything about Summer's stricken face and her use of air quotes told him the experience had been anything but fun.

"No ma'am. No talk necessary." He stood and nervously ran his palms down the front of his shorts before stepping toward Kelly. "I just want you to know I really care about your daughter and I will treat her with respect."

Kelly's smile changed then. It was tender, almost sad; the look of a mother who had toed the worst line of life with her daughter. She gave a nod of her head. "I know you will."

Using her knuckle to dab away a tear, Kelly cleared her throat enthusiastically. "I was coming to talk to you about your birthday dinner."

Parker stopped listening for a few moments after that. His interest suddenly piqued at the reminder of Summer's rapidly upcoming birthday. This was an opportunity Parker knew he had to capitalize on. Summer wasn't the type of girl who wouldn't easily agree to have a fuss made over her, even if she deserved one, but a birthday celebration gave him a window of time to plan something special, something neither of them would forget.

Parker gently interrupted their conversation. "I should probably get home. I have some reading to do before Luke brings dinner."

Summer gave his arm a small squeeze. "Jeopardy later?"

He gave her half a grin. "Of course. I have to be here to keep you from mocking the contestants who answer incorrectly."

"I am not that bad!"

She wasn't but Parker wasn't going to let the chance to leave her all riled up slip by. With a twist of his mouth and a slight shoulder shrug, he left her mood very playfully mussed with.

Taking the same path he took almost daily, he crossed the yard, quickly hopping the fence and jogging slowly up the back porch steps and into his own kitchen. He opened the fridge and pulled out a bottle of Gatorade and an apple on his way to his bedroom to collect his laptop and a notebook.

Once he gathered everything he needed, he sat at the empty dining room table and set himself up to get to work. Taking a healthy bite of the apple, he used one hand to open his laptop prepared to get to work planning for Summer's birthday. The illuminated screen put a halt to his plans. All the still open tabs from his last search were filled with information about congenital heart defects, heart surgeries, and the various prognoses. His own heart squeezed, thumping hard in his chest as he recalled the inundation of information he'd spent hours reading but somehow had left him with even more questions and no real answers.

He'd often think about Summer's condition and feel an overwhelming sense of injustice before reminding himself she was alive, thriving, and defeating the odds stacked against her. And then he would remember the way she looked at him; the way she kissed him and everything was right with the world once again.

Shaking the cloudy thoughts from his mind, Parker opened a new tab on his computer and got busy planning. Parker didn't look up from his screen until the sound of the key turning in the front door called his attention. Checking the time on his phone, he was surprised to see Luke had actually made it home relatively on time.

Parker picked up his pencil to write down the last of the information just as Luke turned into the room, with a brown paper bag that smelled of copious amounts of good food.

"Hey-" Luke's greeting hung there between them

waiting for something else to give it some sort of purpose. Parker shifted uncomfortably in his chair. It seemed neither one of them knew how to tread the safe waters of small talk.

"I didn't think you were going to make it."

Parker's words were true but he did his best to speak them without malice. "The food smells good."

Luke gave Parker a fleeting half smile as he sat the bag down on the table. "I didn't know what you'd like to eat off the menu so I tried to get a good variety."

Parker nodded appreciatively as he closed his laptop and pushed it to the side.

"I'm not interrupting anything too important, am I?"

Parker shook his head. "Nothing I can't finish up later. I'm trying to figure out what to do for Summer's birthday."

"Ah, yes. Summer from next door. She's a sweet girl. If you need any extra funds let me know, birthdays are kind of a big deal right?"

Parker forced his lips to stay shut even as tension flooded his veins. "Since when?"

"I'm sorry?" Luke's unpacking paused in his bewilderment.

"I said, since when have birthdays been a big deal to you? Mine sure weren't."

Luke's hand froze over the carton of beef and broccoli. But Parker didn't feel like waiting for whatever excuse he was going to offer. He'd spent too many birthdays that started with a promise from his dad and ended with his mom making excuses for his preoccupation. Parker had been eight years old the first time he realized his mother signed his father's name on all the cards and gifts she tried to pass off as coming from him. It hadn't been the first time and it definitely wasn't the last.

"I'm sitting here trying to remember a time when you could manage to leave work on time enough to show up to celebrate with me, and I'm coming up short. I mean, even after we left, you couldn't even be bothered enough to stick a card in the mail to show you at least remembered the date."

Parker stood, stacking his book on top of his laptop, tucking both under his arm as he prepared to leave the room. There was a terrible combination of anger and abandonment that swirled around his heart, threatening to steal away any reconciliatory feelings. Memories of spending year after year, watching the door out of the corner of his eye, waiting for his father to walk through.

"Parker, wait a minute."

"I waited for seventeen years!" Parker's voice trembled with buried sentiments that had haunted his thoughts. His eyes burned with tears. "I waited for you to show up and you never did. You never came after me and mom. You just locked yourself up in your office and let us go."

"Son-"

"I can't think of one thing you could say to me right now that I'd be interested in hearing."

Parker walked around the table in effort to make it to his room where he could close the door on all of this. He cringed at the fantasy of a heart broken young boy who still had him hoping maybe things between he and Luke could be salvaged.

"When you turned twelve you had that birthday party at the skate park. You were obsessed with learning how to ride that year. I was there, Parker."

"You're lying."

Luke reached into his pocket and pulled out his wallet. He pulled out several folded and creased pieces of colorful paper invitations. All of which Parker recognized. It knocked the wind out of his lungs.

"I came Parker. I came and I saw how happy you were, happier than you'd ever been living here in Concord. You were happier without me and I decided to stay away after that party, to give you what you deserved."

Parker's laughter burst from his chest almost startling him. He laughed like he hadn't laughed in years while Luke looked on in absolute bewilderment. Oh God, he was losing mind. His parents had officially driven him crazy.

"For someone who makes a career at being smart, that was the dumbest thing I've ever heard."

"I was stupid." Luke slid the old invitations back into his pocket. Shame colored his face. "I had everything a man could want and I didn't just lose it, I chased it away. When your mom packed up and left Parker, it didn't surprise me. I knew I had lost her long before then. The way I neglected her- and you- it's the worst mistake of my life. I've known it every day since."

Parker leaned against the wall, softly banging the back of his head against the smooth surface. "I didn't sign up for this. You two did and you both ended up screwing me over."

Luke nodded. "You're right, Parker. You have the right to be angry and feel hurt. All I'm asking for is a chance."

Parker's mind and heart went to war then. He had never felt as unsure as he felt right then. "A summertime promise can't make for a lifetime of disappointments."

"I know that. I'm willing to do the work. I'll be here for you, Parker."

I'll be here for you.

The words echoed in his mind for the rest of the evening. It pulled at his attention even as Summer's head laid in his lap as they watched TV together.

"You're awful quiet tonight? Did dinner go okay?"

Parker shrugged and ran his fingers through her hair. "It went."

After Luke's plea, Parker had quieted his feelings long enough to sit down to eat. Their conversation sitting like a lead weight in his stomach didn't do his appetite any favors and he hadn't tasted a thing. As soon as he was able to he headed over to Summer's for the comfort he knew just being in her presence would give him.

"I'm sorry it didn't go better for you."

He loved that she didn't feel a need to press him for information. Parker could talk to her about anything, and that included how he felt about his parents. But the truth was, he had packed the day full of doing things he never planned on doing and now he was simply exhausted.

Summer sat up. After a moment of situating herself she patted her lap welcomingly. "Your turn."

Parker gratefully laid his head in her lap. Her delicate fingers instantly went to work, gently playing in his hair. His eyelids grew heavier as her touch lulled him into his dreams.

"I'm here for you, Parker."

chapter Seventeen

Parker strolled rather leisurely alongside Summer as the two of them walked a pair of dogs from the shelter. Realizing if he was going to make an attempt at the whole college thing, he knew she was right about needing some sort of altruistic work on his record. As promised, Mary Ellen had welcomed them back with very excited open arms, and they had spent the day helping clean the kennels and now walking the dogs to get them some exercise and leash practice.

Parker snuck another glance at Summer. He found it worth mentioning how extremely cute she looked that day. Her baseball cap was pulled down low over the two braided pigtails she wore. The yellow t-shirt under the denim overalls she wore reminded him of sunshine.

She shuffled her Converses along the ground trying to keep control of the dog that was easily double her size.

"It's hard to believe the summer is almost halfway over."

Her reminder was true though bittersweet. When he'd first arrived in the sleepy little cul-de-sac, the summer seemed to stretch on into some mundane infinity. He looked down at their interlocked hands. Oh, how things had changed.

"Speaking of your birthday-"

Summer snorted. "We weren't talking about my birthday!"

"Now we are." Playfully winking at her, he brought their hands to his mouth and planted a kiss on the back of her hand. "I made some plans."

"Like what?!"

"I can't tell you all of that just yet. But it does involve a trip to New York City. Do you think your mom would be cool with it?"

Summer's eyes were already dancing at the mere mention of going to the city.

"We can ask her together! I don't think she'd have a problem with it, I mean she walked in on us making out the other day and didn't completely lose her mind."

The thought of that kiss made him smile. Summer rolled her eyes with a shake of her head despite her own knowing grin. It was pretty impossible for him to look at her and not want to kiss her. He wanted to get her alone and make plans to pick up where they had left off.

His ringtone sounded, pulling his mind out of the sweet daydream he was conjuring up. He didn't need to pull it out of his pocket to know who was calling him.

"You're still not going to take her call?"

There was no right answer to the question. He would

never be anything but honest with Summer but if Parker answered honestly then she would just fuss and frown at his reply.

"Life is too short to be angry for so long. Don't you think she's worried about you? You haven't talked to her since the day you came to Concord."

"I guess she shouldn't have shipped me off then."

Summer stopped walking, her lips twisted into a frustrated pout. "She hurt your feelings, I get it. But have you stopped to think if she hadn't sent you to spend the summer here, then we would have never met?"

"I didn't mean it like that, Summer."

He finally stopped walking too. The conversation taking an unexpected detour. Somehow he was getting dangerously close to having a very upset girl on his hands and that was one thing he really didn't need.

"Ending up next door to you was the best thing that could have happened to me, and you're right, for that reason I am grateful for her ultimatum. But that's about the only thing I can say to her that wouldn't make things worse between us. If I answer her call, she's going to ask me about school and I don't want to talk to her about that. I want to talk about how for the first half of my life, I had a father who chose work over me and now that she has Charles…"

Summer took a step closer, lessening the gap between them. Switching the dog leash into her other hand she reached up and cupped his face. "I'm sorry she hurt your feelings."

He squeezed his eyes shut trying to keep control over his emotions. After his breakdown in front of Luke, he didn't want or need a repeat in front of Summer. Sure, he could talk to her about everything, but he wasn't about to willingly loose grip on his emotional control in front of her.

"We should get the dogs back."

She let her hand fall from his face and locked arms with him as they started walking. "I'm sorry for being pushy too."

"Can you repeat that? I want to make sure I get a recording of this moment because I'm positive it will never happen again."

Summer bumped her hip into his side. "Too late. I take it back now."

Parker was waiting on the front porch when Kelly arrived home from work. He figured it was best to talk to her about his idea to celebrate Summer's birthday sooner rather than later in case he needed to go back to the drawing board. Actually taking the time to sit down and plan out something special for a girl was a first and he hoped everything would go as smoothly as he had envisioned. But seeing as how they were only celebrating Summer's seventeenth birthday rather than her eighteenth, it was all dependent on Kelly's approval.

"Good evening, Parker."

Kelly approached him in her teal colored hospital scrubs. Her hair, hair that was oh so similar to Summer's, had been captured into a braid that was draped over her shoulder.

"Something tells me you're wanting to talk to me about something."

"Yes, ma'am."

She pointed a finger in his direction. "Didn't I already tell you about the ma'am stuff? It hasn't changed just because you've taken a liking to my daughter."

Parker smiled sheepishly. The nerves in his stomach were running high. He had spent the last few hours trying to prepare his pitch but suddenly he could barely remember any of what he'd rehearsed.

"I know Summer's birthday is coming up this weekend and I wondered if you would allow me to take her to New York for the day."

"I see." Kelly drew in a deep breath as she sat on the step next to him.

Parker couldn't tell if the 'I see' was good, bad, or indifferent. He gave a quick clearing of his throat and powered forward.

"I thought it would be a fun experience to take the train into the city for the day. I've lived in Brooklyn and went to school there for years before we moved out to Long Island, I promise you I will keep her safe."

Kelly nodded slowly. "I know you would, Parker. It's just... I know she's turning seventeen and graduated, but still all of this is still pretty new to me."

Parker dipped his head in understanding. He didn't know how much Kelly knew about what he knew, but he indeed knew.

The front door flew open then, revealing Summer in one of her favorite oversized t-shirts and a pair of boxer shorts.

"Did you say yes yet?"

"Summer, maybe we can talk about this..."

"Come on, Mom. I never get to do anything this exciting!

I'll be with Parker the whole time and I'll check in as often as you want me to."

Kelly's eyes looked at Summer with love and trepidation battling for prominence in her eyes.

"I'm a big girl now. It's okay for you to let me go."

"It's never been the going that worried me; It's the coming back to me thing that gives me reason to pause."

Summer took a seat in the space on the other side of her mother, hooking her arm around her back. "Please Mama."

Kelly sniffed, blowing out a relenting sigh. "Okay."

Summer's squeal of excitement drowned out the rest of Kelly's words. She placed an exuberant kiss on her mother's cheek.

"You're the best mother in the world."

"And don't you forget it!" Kelly blew a playful raspberry on her daughter's cheek. She stood and collected her work bag. "I'm going to head to bed. It's been a long shift. Lock up when you turn in."

"I will. Goodnight, Mom."

"Goodnight, Kelly... and thank you."

Kelly nodded at him, giving him a tender smile.

As the screen door closed Summer stood, dancing excitedly. "We're going to New York!"

He lightly grabbed her hips steering her to stand in front of him. He felt full of gratitude all of sudden. Grateful for Kelly's blessing. Grateful his father had stayed in that empty house on that quiet cul-de-sac. Above all, he was grateful for the girl standing in front of him. The girl who looked at him as if he had personally hung the moon in the sky. The girl who made him feel like a somebody.

"Thank you."

She raised an eyebrow at him, her smile interrupted by her giggle. "What are you thanking me for? You're the one doing something nice for me."

Parker stood and took gentle hold of her face in both of his hands. He placed a kiss on her forehead, then another on the tip of her nose. "Just thank you."

Her eyes were aglow as if someone had captured stardust and pooled it in her irises. She pulled her bottom lip between her teeth then slowly released it. "You can't be all sweet like that and not expect me to kiss you."

Parker looked to his left and then to his right before offering her a flirtatious smile. "I don't see anyone here stopping you. Go on, kiss me goodnight, Summer."

Parker stared at the screen of his laptop. The main page to begin the application process was open. Ever since his visit to his dad's college, the topic loomed in the peripheral of his focus as if waiting for him to make a decision finally.

The day was soon coming when he would have to figure out the next move for his future, he was just grateful it hadn't arrived just yet. He closed the screen of his laptop, stretching his arms to the side and rolling his neck.

The last couple of days with Summer had been full of the lazy leisure he was used to. They'd spent their days reading in the sunshine and battling for supremacy on whatever video games she decided to explore that day. Now that he was all caught up in calculus, Summer had moved her attention over to pulling the rest of his grades up as well. They'd spent a few hours that evening combing their way through a few of the chapter reviews for his other core subjects, Summer determined to have him start off the year leaps and bounds ahead of where he finished off.

Now back in his own home, Parker paced the floor of his small room. Picking up his phone, he scrolled through his now barely used contacts in search of the name of the one person who could help him pull off his plans.

Richie Gregory had been one of Parker's very first friends when he moved to New York. He'd shown him how to use the transit system and given him a list of the best places to grab egg sandwiches in the morning. But more importantly, he'd been a real friend to Parker. It was the one thing he missed most when he'd been pulled out of Brooklyn by his mom. Even though they weren't able to hang out as often as before, it was a friendship he did his best to maintain.

Now more than ever Parker knew the value of a true friend.

"Parker Reeves! Are you really calling me or am I hallucinating right now?"

Parker chuckled at the greeting. It had been a while since he had talked to Richie but fortunately for him Richie wasn't the type of guy to hold it against him.

"Hey, Rich! I'm going to be coming to the city on Friday. I've got a question for you and I'm really hoping your answer is going to be yes."

Twenty minutes later and in exchange of a promised unnamed future favor, Parker was feeling a lot more confident in what he hoped would be one of the best days of Summer's life.

He put his phone down on the bed and pulled his shirt off tossing it in the direction of his laundry bag.

He'd just shut off the light in his room when he heard the quiet rapping against the glass pane of his window.

"Parker!" The hissed whisper somehow still got his heart racing. The shadowy silhouette of a messy bun. All signs pointed to Summer.

He slid the window open wider. "What are you doing out here?"

"I can't sleep. It's too quiet in my house. Can I come in?"

The confession of her loneliness pulled his heart strings into knots and he immediately reached his hand out helping her climb through the low window into his room.

"You could have asked me to stay if you didn't want to be alone."

She placed her hands squarely on her hips and gave him a cheeky grin. "And exactly what kind of girl do you think I am?"

"Apparently the kind of girl that sneaks into my room late at night instead of just asking me to stay."

"I hope I'm not disturbing you."

Her smile grew wider as her eyes roamed over his bare torso and the sweat shorts that hung low on his hips. His blood rushed through his veins a little bit faster.

If she kept looking at him like that, he was liable to combust with how much energy he was trying to contain.

"I'm going to go and brush my teeth. Make yourself comfortable. We'll watch a movie or something when I'm through."

"What about Luke?"

"He's sleeping. He won't bother us."

Ten minutes later, Parker had Summer in his arms as they lay on his bed. It was far more comfortable with a beautiful girl in his company.

"Do you think your Mom will come over here looking for you in the morning?"

"She won't be back until lunchtime."

So, he would be able to have her in his arms for the entire night. That worked for him. He pulled her against him tightly.

"I'm going to ask you a question but I don't want you to feel like you have to answer it if you don't want to."

"'Kay." She rolled over to face him. Their faces were so close their lips brushed as she whispered.

"Do you ever think about your dad?"

She blinked as she took a sharp inhale. "All the time. I think about what a piece a garbage he is and how my life is so much better without him."

Her smirk couldn't mask the tenderness behind her words.

"That's what I mean. Have you ever thought about telling him to his face? You know, for closure?"

Summer sighed. "I used to. I tracked him down one year. He lives about twenty minutes from here, go figure. Turned out he got himself a brand new wife and two brand new fully heart functional kids. Suddenly I didn't feel like wasting my breath on him anymore."

He pressed a caring kiss to her lips.

"I know what you're thinking. Don't you dare apologize for his mistakes, Parker."

Chapter Eighteen

Two voices greeted Parker as he walked through the back door of Summer's house. One was nervous: the other agitated. He recognized the agitated one immediately.

"99.9 is barely a fever, Mom."

"Only one of us went to school to be a nurse as far as I know."

"I want a second opinion. I'm your daughter, it's a complete conflict of interest." Summer huffed. He could feel her exaggerated eye roll in the energy.

He cleared his throat to announce his presence. Summer gestured wildly in the air. "Parker! Please tell my mother she's being unreasonable."

One glance at Kelly's face told him that would be the absolute worst thing he could say to her right then. He had enough parental problems as it was, adding another one would be volunteering for a slow death at this point. He offered her a commiserating wince instead, placing a comforting hand on her back.

"What's going on?"

Kelly waved the thermometer she held in her hand. "Summer is running a fever. I'm not sure going to New York in the morning is such a good idea anymore."

"Yeah, except I'm not sick. It's barely a fever. I'll take a dose of Tylenol and be ready go."

Concern muddled his excitement. He wanted to go to New York almost as much as Summer did but he wasn't about to risk something as valuable as her health to get there. He placed a palm to her forehead only to be fiercely swatted away.

"I'm not sick!" Summer's eyes narrowed at him. "I'm going to New York tomorrow."

She spun on her heel and pushed her way through the screen door, letting it slam behind her as she punished the ground beneath her feet on her way to the shed.

The troubled mood she'd left in the air seem to permeate everything. Kelly suddenly looked decades older as they shuffled around the emotional bomb that had just been detonated. The sound of the oven timer going off cut through the heavy silence.

"Well, dinner's done."

She dropped the thermometer to the table, walking over to the oven to pull out the roast chicken. Her shoulders sagged as she set the pan on the cooling rack. Parker started to take a step forward then stopped himself. He didn't know if there was anything he could do that would make her feel better.

"I never meant to cause any trouble."

"You didn't." Kelly sniffed, swiping at her cheek. "Even though I'm right, she's right too; I have to let her go."

He dipped his head, running his hand through his hair. "I know I'm only seventeen, but I know a good parent when I see one. You're a great mom, Kelly."

She looked at him with grateful watery eyes. Her thanks was whispered but it echoed loudly in his heart.

"Is it safe to come in?"

Parker dipped his head into the open entryway of Summer's shed. He found her laying on her back. Her hands resting behind her head, she stared at the ceiling, or maybe she was staring through the ceiling, those probing eyes of hers always did seem to see beyond things.

"I'll apologize to her later."

She didn't look at him as he stepped fully into the room. He lay next to her, fixing his gaze at her profile. He wanted to smile at her, because looking at her always had that effect on him, but he didn't. Instead, he just lay with her. She deserved to have whatever time she needed to feel whatever she needed to feel.

"I've spent most of my life wondering why I'm sick, when I'm going to get sick, and of course actually being too sick to do anything. I'm not giving this up."

Summer had fought for years to just be a normal teenager, and in Parker's eyes she was. Even knowing the story behind her scar, it was often too easy to forget she wasn't a typical teenage girl. She'd fought long and hard to get to this point where she just wanted to hop on a train and go spend the day in the city where the boy next door could make her feel as special as she'd made him feel.

This was one of those times where he remembered.

The trembling of her voice revealed a vulnerability he

knew she tried not to show often. It was a gift he recognized and one he wanted to never take for granted.

"Okay. Then we're going." He squeezed her hand. "But I need you to promise me something. If you do feel sick, I need you to tell me."

He could see the argument in her eyes. She opened her mouth to protest but he cut her off with a quick kiss.

"Just humor me, then. Please."

"Fine." She ran her tongue across the seam of her lips. "I promise."

"Good. I care about you, Summer."

The racing of his heart told him it was an understatement. In reply, she turned into him resting her head on his shoulder and draping her arm over his torso. She cared about him too. He could feel it in her touch. He could taste in her kiss. He could hear it in her voice every time she coerced him to do something about his future and he saw it in her eyes every time she looked at him.

He was in it deeply with this girl.

"Thanks for the ride."

Parker adjusted the straps of his backpack as he stood on the sidewalk in front of the train station. Summer happily stood by his side, her own back pack on her back and two cups of iced coffee in hand. She'd been fever free and rearing to go since she showed up on his porch that morning looking cuter than anyone should look at seven o'clock in the morning.

He didn't know it was humanly possible to make a pair of denim shorts and a fitted tee shirt look as incredible as she made them look.

Luke gave him a small but earnest smile as he nodded his head. "Of course. I hope you both have a good day, and Parker... call me, you know, if you need anything."

"Okay."

The awkwardness between them seemed magnified under Summer's intrigued gaze. It was time to wrap this up.

"Well, we need to get going. Our train is going to be leaving soon."

He took one of the cups of coffee from Summer's hand, freeing it up so he could intertwine their fingers together. They were almost through the doors when Luke's voice called Parker back to him.

"I want you to take this and keep it. I set up this account a long time ago. It's got a lot of birthday money in it."

Luke pressed a brand new debit card in his hand and then with an apologetic smile he returned to his car and pulled away from the curb. Parker turned the card over in his hand a few times before tucking it into his pocket. If it was an attempt at buying redemption, it wouldn't be that easy. Still, Parker wasn't about to turn down money, especially when he was about to take his girl to the city.

The last time he'd rode the train, he'd been heading to Concord with more troubles than he knew what to deal with and a bad attitude to boot. It was funny how time changed things. No. He looked over at Summer who smiled wistfully as the trees whizzed past them. It was funny how she changed things.

"Are you still not going to tell me what we're doing today?"

Parker pretended to think about it for a minute before shaking his head. The element of surprise was going to be his biggest weapon in making this day special. So far, everything was going smoothly and he needed to ensure it continued that way.

"All I can say is that I kind of plan on kissing you a lot."

The roll of her eyes was watered down by her happy grin. He buried his fingers in the soft waves of her hair, tucking it behind her ear as he leaned in. Brushing his lips with hers softly, he relished the quick intake of breath she took in anticipation for his kiss.

"Happy birthday, Summer."

Walking up the ramp to Grand Central Station was something he'd probably done close to a hundred times. But watching Summer's face come alive with awe as they stepped under the majestic dome made it feel more special than it ever had. Instantly surrounded by the constant hum of conversation and people scurrying from one place to the other was the tell-tale sign they weren't in Concord anymore.

"There's so many people."

"You haven't seen anything yet." He grabbed her hand securely and confidently wove their way through people until they pushed out one of the doors. The sounds of the city made him smile as he stepped near the curb and stuck his hand out to hail the next cab. "Welcome to New York sweetheart!"

To her credit, Summer put up no arguments as they climbed into the backseat of the cab. Her excitement of being in the city apparently outweighed her trepidation at riding with strangers. She sat close to him, her legs pressed against his as his hand cupped her bare knee.

"In case I forget to tell you later, thanks for the best birthday ever."

God, this girl made him feel in ways he never knew were possible. He hadn't known how it could feel, to find someone you wanted to be with more than anyone else in the world. No one told him how it could be.

He placed a kiss to her temple. He couldn't take the risk of kissing her the way he wanted to. If he kissed her the way he kissed her in the private moment on the train, they might have ended up walking the rest of the way to Brooklyn.

He had the cab pull over a few blocks away from their destination wanting to give Summer a bit of a tour of his old neighborhood. She happily listened as she snapped pictures of the skylines and anything else she deemed memorable. Parker looked on happily, thankful he'd brought extra packs of film for her camera.

The smell of Shake Shack filled the air and caused his stomach to rumble. Due to meet Richie a little while later, he checked the time on his phone. "Are you hungry?"

"I could eat."

"Oh, thank God." Parker eagerly took her hand and quickly led her in the direction of food as she laughed without restraint.

Burgers, shakes, and Summer. It was the recipe for happiness.

He snapped a picture of her as she took a healthy sip of her strawberry shake, her eyes aglow with contentment. He posted it to his Instagram without a thought of hesitation.

    @ParkerReeves: my home SWEET home

She raised a curious eyebrow at the goofy smile he wore as the first of the speculating comments began to appear. Wiping the corners of her mouth with a napkin she bounced a little in her seat. "So, that was pretty amazing. What's next on the agenda?"

He didn't know if it was possible to prepare anyone for the force of nature that Richie was. The best he could offer was a roguish smirk and a shoulder shrug. "You'll see."

chapter nineteen

Leading Summer up the stairs to Richie's apartment felt a little like leading a lamb into a wolf den. The boisterous sounds of laughter could be heard through the shut door before Parker knocked.

"Remember I told you about the one decent friend I had left?"

She nodded. Her eyes were both curious and excited.

"Well, brace yourself. You're about to meet Richie Gregory."

No sooner had he warned her of the tornado of pure energy headed their way did the door swing open wildly.

"Parker Reeves!" Richie's enthusiastic greeting came complete with a back-slapping hug.

Richie looked almost the same as the last time that Parker had saw him. No, seriously, he might have been wearing the same exact t-shirt, the one that declared he was a hug dealer. Richie's perfect smile turned towards

Summer. Standing at just about six feet tall and made up of muscle he somehow got from eating pizza and burritos all day, Richie's presence had the ability to demand attention. From the look on her face as she looked him up and down, Summer's attention was demanded.

"And you must be the beautiful Summer. C'mon in."

Richie's arm found a resting spot over her shoulders as he escorted him into the apartment. Apparently their reunion was set to be trumped by an introduction to a beautiful girl. Parker frowned in amused disbelief as he closed the door behind him.

"Welcome to my casa."

He placed their backpacks on the floor near the door and scanned the room. Fortunately, the apartment was in a fairly livable state with only one pizza box resting on the counter. Bright and edgy concert posters lined the walls of the small space while a guitar and several amps took up the available space in the corner. Several bodies littered the sofa as a raucous round of gaming consumed their attention.

"Summer, these are my roomies. Lance, Corey, TJ, say hello to Summer."

Distracted hellos replied in unison.

Summer brought her hand to her lips trying to tamp down her amused smile.

"Ignore them." Richie picked up a lock of her hair and examined it. "I must say, you have some of the best hair I've ever seen."

Another smile and round of giggles. "Thanks, I grew it myself."

"Can I get you something to drink? Or something to eat?

Or maybe you'd like somewhere to rest, my bed is awful comfortable."

"Dude!"

If Parker had been so blatant, Summer would have a written up a list of the places where he could shove the idea. So, he was a little dumbfounded to see her give him one of those incredible smiles of hers that would make you feel like the greatest. Parker crossed his arms over his chest. He'd heard enough.

"You do see me standing here, don't you?"

Richie looked from Parker to Summer and then back again. "Oh! So when you said you were bringing your girl, you didn't mean your home girl?"

"I meant my girl as in *my* girl." Parker took hold of Summer's hand and pulled her into his arms. With her back against his chest, he wrapped his arms around her hips with the familiarity of someone who had held her plenty of times before.

Richie solemn face dissolved into laughter. "Oh man, you should see your face right now! I'm just joshing with you."

Summer's shoulders shook with hilarity.

"Oh, you think that's funny?" He wanted to promise payback. But then she looked up at him and all his threatening thoughts turned to promises of kissing her until she would be too breathless to try and tease him. She caught her lip between her teeth, still taunting him.

Richie cleared his throat dramatically. His eyes were lit with amusement. "Do you both need my bed? It's getting a little hot in here."

Summer's cheeks did turn pink with color then. He

wondered if it was because she was thinking the same thing he was then. He kissed her neck quickly.

"So Rich, did you get that thing I asked you about?"

"Yep. It's en route. Benny is putting the finishing touches on it."

"Great. We have an appointment we need to get to so I need you to take care of the business end of things. Make sure the product is right though, I don't want any of that crap he gave to Joey." Parker pulled out his wallet and handed Richie a crisp one-hundred-dollar bill.

As soon as Richie excused himself to make a phone call, Summer turned to face him. As she twisted her face in question and put her hands on her hips he knew what was coming next.

"Parker Reeves, what on earth is going on?"

"We're crossing another thing off your list and getting you a fake ID."

Summer's wide eyes were torn between confusion and delight. "What? How? Seriously?"

"Richie and I know a guy."

"Should I be concerned that you know a guy who can just whip up fake documentation?"

"Only if I should be concerned about why you need one. I mean you're the one who put it on your list."

She shrugged her shoulders and took a seat on one of the kitchen stools. "I just wanted one, like one of the cool kids."

"Well I'm getting you one sweetheart. And then maybe, just maybe, we'll put it to use."

"Is that what the appointment is about?"

The appointment.

He pulled her to her feet. "We need to get going actually. Grab your pocket book and camera. We can leave the rest of the stuff here. I'm going to go tell Richie we're heading out for a bit."

"Hey, Parker?"

"Yeah?"

She cocked her hip to the side and tapped a polished pink fingernail on her chin. "So why exactly did you have a fake ID?"

Parker gave her a guilty smirk.

After a quick subway ride, it was time to unveil the next part of the day he'd planned for Summer. To his relief, she hadn't picked at him for any clarification of the murky parts of his past that had resulted in him acquiring a guy who could supply him with some of the best fake identification cards out there. Truth be told, while his purpose behind the card wasn't completely delinquent driven, she would have still lambasted him once again for his choice of past associates. It was a lesson he'd learned the hard way.

As they neared the address Parker felt his eagerness kick up a few levels. He'd always thought the whole 'giving is better than receiving' thing was a bit of a crock. Until Summer that is. It was yet another thing he could say she taught him. The idea that she would be happy with what was about to happen was enough to make him smile until his face hurt.

"So, I was looking through your list as I was planning

this day and I saw this thing about getting a tattoo…"

Summer stopped walking in the middle of the sidewalk, which was a hazard in New York. He quickly pulled her to the side as she squealed excitedly.

"A tattoo!"

For someone who had put up quite a fuss when he pulled out a straight pin to remove a splinter from her foot she was way too excited about the idea of getting permanently altered by a needle. He did his best to keep his face straight. "Calm down and close your eyes. Don't open them until I tell you."

She muttered something about him being so bossy all of a sudden but her smile was too big for him to take her complaint seriously. Once he was satisfied she wasn't peeking, he safely led her along the sidewalk for a few more yards. Coming to a stop in front of a brick building, he read the large store front window before escorting Summer inside.

"Okay, open your eyes."

He watched as she scanned the room taking in the art lining the walls. "Where are we?"

"It's a Henna Tattoo Salon. You get your tattoo to cross off your list and I get to live to see my next birthday since your mom won't kill me because I brought you home permanently inked."

Her eyes pooled with tears and Parker's heart stuttered in his chest. He wondered if he'd planned this totally wrong. He never wanted to disappoint her but now he wondered if straddling the line between her and Kelly had been a precarious situation to put himself in.

"Hey, you okay? I promise next year for your eighteenth

we'll do the real thing if you still want to..."

She shut him up with a kiss. "This is perfect, Parker."

"You're happy?"

"The happiest I've ever been."

Their moment was interrupted by the appearance of a beautiful young Indian woman. Her smile was wide and welcoming as she approached them.

"Welcome, my name is Neha."

Parker shook her hand politely. "Hi, we spoke on the phone. I'm Parker and this is Summer. I made an appointment."

"Ah, yes. Please come with me." She placed a warm hand on Summer's arm and led her over to a comfortable chaise.

Neha spent several minutes fussing over Summer, ensuring that she was comfortable and insisting they both accept a cup of tea before she settled into work. Parker couldn't help but to keep sneaking looks over at the warm glow that illuminated Summer's face as she talked with Neha about the type of design she wanted.

"I'm paying. Get whatever you want." Parker reminded her.

"Parker, you've already done so much for me."

"I'm just getting started. Sit back, relax, and enjoy your birthday."

As Neha went to work, she and Summer talked about the history of traditional henna and the culture that surrounded it while Parker documented the process through photos and video. He watched Neha skillfully decorate Summer's hand and begin working her way up her arm.

The buzzing of his phone alerted him to the next part of his plan.

"You think you'll be okay here for a bit? I need to go meet a friend to pick up something we need for later. I'll be gone for thirty minutes at most."

"I'm guessing you're not going to tell me about that plan either then?"

"Of course not."

"I'll be fine, Parker."

He took her free hand in his and kissed it. "Maybe you can give your mother a call while I step out."

"Fine. I'll check in."

"That's my girl."

Another kiss to her hand and Parker excused himself. He made it to the corner before he changed his pace. He had to squeeze an hour's worth of errands into thirty minutes.

You know what was the best feeling in the world?

Having someone look genuinely ecstatic to see you when you walk into a room. Summer beamed brightly as he stepped back into the cozy parlor. She sat with her arm extended the stunningly intricate design now drying while Neha smiled softly at him from where she now worked on another customer.

"Parker, you're back!"

"Of course, I am." He came close to her, pressing a kiss to her forehead. "Now let me see how it looks."

Summer's complete half sleeve mehndi design was

complex, sophisticated, and intrinsically gorgeous. Just like her. Neha had taken care that even the smallest of details had been placed perfectly her skin.

"You like it?"

Parker needed to make sure she did since this day was about her after all. He looked up to find her gaze fixed on him in a way that made him wish he could see what she was seeing.

"I love it."

Her eyes said more than the simple words she spoke. His own unspoken thoughts rose to the surface again. There in the middle of a small shop in Brooklyn he could feel the very moment she had tilted his world yet again.

"Ready to go?"

"Almost." He shrugged off his backpack and retrieved her camera. "Smile for the camera."

Nabbing the shot to add to her board, he insisted she pose for another taken on his phone. Only after he'd captured her face in different stages of amused impatience did he extend a hand out to her which she quickly took. The way their palms fit together so perfectly Parker wondered if anything could feel better.

Then he looked at her mouth and remembered.

This girl did things to him.

"How are you feeling? You tired? Need anything?"

Summer didn't know the rest of his plans for the day but he did. His promise to take care of her wasn't just lip service to Kelly, he'd made the promise to himself well before. It was one he intended to keep.

"I'm good. Are we going back to Richie's place?"

"Nope. I had something else in mind."

Not wanting to bring her on the subway again so soon after getting such a beautiful piece created on her arm, he stuck his arm out in the air confidently calling the next available cab over.

"Get in. I'll tell you on the way."

Parker gave the driver instructions before settling in besides Summer. He reached into his pocket and pulled out two tickets he handed over to her. They'd be crossing yet another item off her list in just few more hours.

"This is where we're going tonight. A buddy of mine brought the tickets for me earlier this week, I had to go meet with him to pick them up."

"I've never been to a concert before!"

"I know." He chuckled. "That's why I'm taking you. But first, we're going shopping. You're going to pick out whatever you want to wear tonight, and then I'm going to try and look at least as half as good."

Her lips formed a perfect 'o' of surprise. "You are not spending any more money on me."

Using his thumb and forefinger he tipped her chin up to bring her lips to his. He delivered a soft and quick kiss. "Oh, but I am. I'm taking you out for a birthday dinner too."

"I can't let you pay for all of this. I feel like I'm just taking and taking."

"You haven't taken anything that I'm not offering. If I could, I would give you the world, Summer."

chapter Twenty

Parker paced the floor of Richie's apartment. Summer had excused herself to borrow the bathroom and shower to prepare for their dinner date. Being in New York, most girls would have seized the opportunity of going shopping and have dragged him to the most expensive stores they could find. Not Summer, though. After he finally got her to stop arguing with him about the whole thing she then decided to make it hard for him to spoil her as she became the world's most frugal shopper. The whole thing would make him laugh later when he wasn't actively trying to spoil this girl.

"Hey, Joey just called. He's on his way with the card."

"Thank goodness." Parker rubbed his hands together anxiously.

With a grin playing on his face, Richie reached into the fridge and pulled out a beer. "Want one? You look like you need it."

He was definitely nervous. It was silly considering he'd

basically been with Summer all day and every day for weeks now. But there was something weightier about taking her out to dinner that made his palms sweatier and his heart race in anticipation as he waited for her to walk down the narrow hallway.

He turned his attention back to the bottle of beer Richie held out in his direction. Parker hadn't drank since he went to Concord. After he met Summer, he hadn't missed it at all. "Nah, I'm good."

Richie nodded easily. "I figured. You're different, Parker."

"Am I?"

"Yep and I'm betting that girl in there is a big part of the reason why."

Parker couldn't argue with the truth. "She's special."

Richie pulled out a cold piece of pizza from a nearby box. "I can tell. Good for you."

He felt Summer's presence before he saw her. Of course, there was also Richie's low whistle of appreciation that tipped him off. But still, nothing could have prepared him for how good she looked.

The soft pink fitted spaghetti strap dress she wore fit her slender curves like a second skin and she had traded in her neon sneakers for a pair of dainty sandals that made her legs look more amazing than usual. Her hair had been brushed and captured into a tidy bun, and he admired the gentle and elegant slope of her neck. She draped the gauzy floral kimono over her arm as she walked near to him, blushing under his fervent gaze.

He couldn't help it. Something as beautiful as she was deserved to be thoroughly considered. He was just getting started.

"Well aren't you going to say something?" She subconsciously rubbed at the exposed bit of her scar.

"I don't know what to say- "

Summer's smile wobbled then and he didn't care about Richie sitting just a foot away from them, or the fact that any second now they were bound to be interrupted when Joey arrived with her I.D. in hand. He didn't care about anyone or anything except making sure she felt as beautiful as she looked.

He pulled her hand away from her scar and onto the back of his neck just before he pulled her into his kiss. "You're so beautiful, sweetheart. I'm the luckiest guy in the world."

"You think?"

He shook his head, the corner of his mouth curling up into a smile as he ran his tongue over his lips. "I know."

The doorbell buzzed just then. Joey's impeccable timing reminding Parker that as much as he wanted to just sit there alternating between kissing Summer and staring at her, they had somewhere to be.

Dinner couldn't have gone more perfectly. He couldn't have picked a better way to use some of the funds his father had handed over that morning.

Since their transition from a simple friendship, kissing and physical displays of affection had never been a problem for them. But taking her away for the day gave him the opportunity to show her some romance. Having dinner at a restaurant that gave them a stunning view of the city skyline and river while nature basked them in the glow of the setting sun? Yeah, it couldn't get much better than that.

Now as they made their way deeper into the concert venue, Parker gave himself a small thumbs up as Summer enthused over how much fun she'd had so far. They had a few more hours left in this day and he was resolved to finish strong. Her happiness meant his success, and Parker had never wanted to succeed so badly before.

Summer admired her altered identification card for the third or fourth time since the bouncer had let them in. "I can't believe they let us in!"

Parker placed a hand over her mouth, playfully hushing her. "They can still kick us out you know."

A round of effervescent giggles escaped her. "Sorry, I'm just so excited."

"I'm excited that you're excited. Now let me take your picture, we have to cross this off the list properly."

She did as he asked before demanding his phone. "Let's take one for your gram thingy."

"Instagram." He corrected her with a chuckle. He knew she knew exactly what it was. Though she still remained adamant that she didn't want an account for herself, over the last few weeks, she'd become more and more interested in scrolling through his feed of pictures and asking questions about the people he followed and interacted with.

He quickly agreed, handing over the phone. Stepping behind her, he wrapped his arms around her waist like they belonged there and pulled her into him. Warmth flooded him and it felt like fire coursed through his veins; he felt...

After months of just going the motions of living. He actually felt alive. It felt incredible.

The crowd whooped with excitement as the band took the stage. Summer immediately joined in with such a fervor that Parker wondered if she was more excited about the whooping than the actual band. It had only taken about half a song before she was dancing like she was the only one in the room.

And of course, she was captivating.

Watching her move in ways he'd never seen her move before made it nearly impossible to do anything else. Her zest was infectious. The more she moved the more he wanted to. It was easy to lose himself in the music alongside her.

So, he did.

He fell with her and along the way he finally found the words to explain the way his heart raced whenever he was around her and the way his soul craved her when they were apart; the way she made him feel... everything.

"I love this song!" She shouted over the reverberating bass pulsing through the air.

He just smiled because he already knew. She had played it on repeat for nearly an entire day the past week. She beamed a blissful smile in his direction before she closed her eyes and swayed to the music.

The lead singer stopped singing then, mopping his brow as he scanned the crowd. "Anyone out there know the words to this song?"

Summer's eyes flew open just as Parker's grin went roguish. They exchanged glances for half a second before Parker started calling attention to her. Her furious objections were glazed with her hysterics.

And then, because the moon and stars had apparently aligned in his favor, the singer pointed his microphone directly at her and asked security to help her get to the stage. Not only had they successfully infiltrated the concert, but now Summer was crashing the actual stage. He did what every supportive guy in his position would do, he readied the camera.

She took the stage all the while shooting him the most adorable incredulous look he had ever seen as the packed crowd erupted into cheers and whistles. Her hand automatically flew to her chest rubbing at the scar that no one was looking at.

Parker gave her a nod of encouragement. She took with a wink, drawing in a deep breath as she took the microphone. A strange hush fell over the lively crowd them, almost as if they knew the same thing that he knew.

Something special was about to happen.

The fact that she could sing shouldn't have surprised him. He had yet to find one thing she wasn't at least decent at. But singing would be a massive understatement for what happened next. When Summer opened her mouth, magic spilled out. His skin erupted into goosebumps as he shouted in appreciation. Slowly her hand fell away from her chest as she sang, her voice was downright heavenly as she matched the melody.

The crowd was loving her.

He was loving her…

He was in love with her.

chapter Twenty One

Parker stood back as Richie embraced Summer, lifting her feet off the ground as he squeezed her into a giant bear hug. It was nice to see two of the very few people he considered loyal friends get along so perfectly.

"Thanks for letting us crash your pad today. Maybe you'll come to Concord one day? I can show you around my hood."

Parker snorted. "By 'hood' she means the quietest neighborhood in the history of the 'burbs."

"Hey! It gets pretty vicious out there when the raccoons and skunks have a turf war going on."

"Maybe I will. Do me a favor?"

"Of course." She replied, a curious glint making her eyes shine.

"Take care of this guy for me."

Summer looked at him then. Her eyes filled with something he so desperately wanted to call love. She reached out and took his hand in hers. "I'll do my best."

Richie planted a friendly kiss on her cheek before giving Parker the over complicated yet traditional handshake of theirs. They didn't need to say the words the other already knew. "Get home safe."

Home.

He looked at Summer's contented face and she hugged his arm. He was already there.

The train ride home was quiet. With his arm around her shoulders and the train rocking her to sleep, Summer dozed against him as he kept them safe. She still wore her dress from the concert but her sandals had been packed away into her backpack and her sneakers were back on. Loose tendrils of hair escaped her bun and every so often he would hear her mutter something about Jeopardy in her sleep.

She was perfect.

As the train crossed into Connecticut, Parker quietly called Luke, who thankfully agreed to meet them at the station to give them a ride home. He didn't know if things between him and his father could ever be truly mended, if he would ever be able to know his dad would show up for him, but if Summer hadn't taught him anything else, she had taught him there was always time to try something new and one of the first things on his forming list was to give Luke a chance.

Summer was awake but just as quiet as they rode in the back seat of Luke's Subaru. As Luke drove them along the empty streets, the jazz music he played filled the silence of the car with its languid sound. She gently rubbed her thumb along his, their hands locked together as she rested her head on his shoulder.

Luke pulled into the driveway of their house as Parker looked over at Summer's darkened house. Kelly would be at work until morning.

"Thanks for the ride. I'm going to walk Summer home and make sure she gets in safely."

Summer echoed his thanks, giving Parker's hand a squeeze of appreciation.

Despite the time on the clock and the long day of activity their walk was unhurried. It had been nice being in the city, surrounded by the familiar rushed pace of life, but even he had to admit it was nice to come back to Concord where the starry sky wasn't washed out by the bright city lights. Even in Long Island for the past year, he'd never slowed down enough to remember to just look up and take it all in sometimes.

But that was before Summer.

"Did you have fun today?"

Seeing her tell-tale smile was all the reassurance he needed, but hearing the words were extra special. "I had the best day ever. I can't wait to look through all the pictures tomorrow, er, I mean today."

He took her hips in his hands and gently lifted her onto her steps bringing her eye to eye with him. He had so much he'd been holding inside for so long, he was ready to share it with the one person he could trust with it.

"I've got one more thing to give you. I've been holding onto it for a while now trying to find the right time to give it to you. Now that we're standing here where things kind of started for us, it finally feels right."

Summer's face was washed over with confusion as he dug into his pocket and produced a little velvet satchel. Gently shaking the content of the bag into his palm revealed the peridot ring she'd admired weeks ago at the fair. The realization filled her eyes with tears.

"Parker! When? How?"

"This ring belongs on your hand, I couldn't let anyone else have it. So, I brought it... and I hope you wear it and remember this summer... and that you remember me."

A solitary tear rolled down her cheek. She wrapped her arms around him and kissed him soft and long. "I could never forget you."

"Good. Because I'm in love with you, Summer. You're the best friend I've ever had and I am completely in love with you. If you could find it in your heart to ever think of me the way I think about you, I promise you I won't break your heart..."

She snickered and gestured at her chest. "Too late for that."

"Summer." He gave her a warning look, shaking his head at her gallows humor. "Look, I don't expect you to feel the same way or anything."

"Don't be stupid. Of course, I love you."

Parker squeezed his eyes shut for a second, willing this moment to imprint on his brain forever. He didn't want to forget anything about it. Not the way she looked in the moonlight, nor the way she felt as she pressed herself against him, and especially not the words she said.

No one besides his mother had ever told him he was loved. More than that, for the first time in a long time, he felt the truth in the words. "You love me?"

"Without a doubt."

Kissing her with every bit of everything he felt right then, Parker slid the ring on her finger. "Happy birthday, sweetheart."

Chapter Twenty Two

He had to take her out on a real honest to goodness date.

Parker had come to this conclusion as he sat watching her play video games. Nothing about their relationship had felt traditional but now things between them were growing more serious, and he felt the need to make sure he gave her proper consideration. She hadn't had any of the same opportunities to experience young romance as most of their peers had, Parker couldn't let this one slip through their grasp.

"Are you free tomorrow evening?"

Summer raised a confused eyebrow in his direction. "Why are you asking me that question?"

"Because I want to know if you're available!" He tried to keep a straight face.

She paused the game, setting the controller aside. She turned to face him, regarding him with a probing perusal. Wagging a finger in his direction she smirked, "You're up to something."

"Me? Up to something? Never!"

"Well then why do you want to suddenly know about my plans?"

He tucked her hand in his, gently rubbing his thumb over her knuckles, admiring the way the ring he'd given her complimented her slender fingers. "You can never make it easy on me can you?"

"After all this time, why should I start now?" The playful sparkle in her eyes was tinted with affection. The girl did have a point.

"I want to know if you're free because that's what people normally do before they ask the other person out on a date."

"A date?"

"Yeah you know, I'll come to your house with flowers, take you out on the town, figure out if you'll let me get to second base..."

She punched his shoulder. "You're so annoying."

"So, what do you say? Can I take you out tomorrow?"

She pursed her lips for a second before leaning in and planting a kiss on his cheek. "Of course you can."

Getting Summer to say yes without divulging his entire plan for the evening was only half of his battle. After wooing her in New York, he wanted to replicate the same magic of that day in Concord. So, after waiting for Luke to get home that night, he decided to do the one thing he never imagined doing. He had to ask his father for a favor.

Standing rather awkwardly in the kitchen doorway, Parker realized it would have been much easier to ask a favor from someone he actually talked to on a regular basis. He cleared his throat drawing Luke's attention from the pile of mail he sorted through.

"Oh, hey Parker, I didn't hear you come in." Crossing his ankles, he took his glasses off, sitting them to rest on top of the island before leaning against the counter.

"Guess all those ninja classes I took have paid off."

Luke's perplexed expression was enough to make Parker burst into laughter. "It was a joke."

"Oh, right, of course." He nervously laughed. "I guess I need to take up a few comedy classes, huh?"

Parker inwardly winced. Dad jokes were the worst. "So, uh, I was wondering if I could borrow your car tomorrow night? I want to take Summer out on a date and the whole bike thing is cramping my style."

A more relaxed smile came over Luke's face now. "So, you two have been spending a lot of time together. Things getting more serious?"

Parker weighed how badly he didn't want to have this conversation against how badly he needed a car for his date. "I guess you could say that."

Luke gave a nod of his head. "I can be home around six thirty tomorrow. Will that work for you?"

Parker grinned excitedly. "That's perfect. Thanks, Luke."

"Yeah, uh, no problem." Luke ran a hand over his chin. "Hey, Parks, I was thinking about heading out to one of my favorite Turkish restaurants for dinner. They make an awesome kabob. You want to come?"

"I already ate dinner with Summer and Kelly."

He could almost feel Summer's nudging him in the ribs. She was officially becoming the voice of his conscience. There was a wall of hesitation built up around the part of his brain that could have easily agreed to the invitation and Parker didn't know how to break it down.

"Maybe I could take a rain check?"

The room to hope was enough to return the smile to his father's face. He nodded and returned the glasses to his face. "Another time then."

The next day flew by in a haze. With Summer off with her mom for most of the day, Parker was left to his own devices which meant he spent a lot of time being bored as he stalked the clock. He dragged himself through the practice tests Summer had so conveniently emailed him the links to before he started the preparations for the evening.

He'd hung out with this girl nearly every day but this would be their first official date and he didn't want to skip any of the steps. So, by the time he heard Luke pull into the garage, he'd already been downtown to get a haircut, picked up some flowers and got home in time to iron his shirt.

When he knocked on Summer's door he felt oddly nervous. He shifted from one foot to the other wondering if there would ever be a time when this girl didn't send his emotions into overdrive. As the door opened and revealed her standing there in an olive-green tank dress, her hair blown out into sleek and shiny strands, and the deep pink stain of lip gloss making her mouth even more irresistible. She wore a pair of all white Converse sneakers that couldn't have been more perfect. He couldn't stop smiling.

"You look great." They both spoke in unison before tumbling into a fit of laughter.

He held out a simple bouquet of wildflowers. It was the only bunch that seemed fitting for Summer's spirit. She was everything wild and colorful, but still felt like home. Watching her take them and smile, reassured him that he had made the right choice.

"These are beautiful, Parker." Freeing a daisy stem she made quick work of tucking it behind her ear.

She was beautiful.

"You ready to go?" He dangled the car keys in front of her. "I've got the car tonight."

Throwing a goodbye to her mother over her shoulder she set the flowers on the small table in the entry way before taking his hand and closing the door behind her as they left. Parker led her to the parked Subaru, sneaking a small kiss before he opened the passenger side door for her and revealed her waiting camera. He had taken a small detour to her shed to retrieve it before their date.

Summer waited until he put the key into the ignition before she pounced. "So where are we going?"

"Geez girl, you waste no time do you?" Grinning, he shook his head. "You're pretty good with trivia, right?"

"I do alright." Her humble brag was marked by a smirk.

"Tell me, do you know how many drive in movies are still in operation?"

"Uh-"

Parker didn't wait for her to respond as he put the car into gear. "I don't really know the answer to that, so it doesn't matter. What does matter is the fact that I saw a certain girl who I just so happen to love put going to one on her list. As fate would have it, I found one still in operation a couple of towns over."

She smiled excitedly.

"I'm taking you to the movies, sweetheart."

In the privacy of their own car, with Summer cuddled into his side, her dress riding up to bare the smooth golden tanned skin of those legs he loved, Parker couldn't figure out why these drive-in movie things weren't popular anymore.

"Are you watching the movie?" She whispered conspiratorially.

"I'm trying to but somebody keeps asking me if I'm watching the movie every two seconds."

She wrinkled her nose at him, bunching up all her freckles and looking adorable enough to eat... or something along those lines. Taking the daisy from her hair she rolled it between her forefinger and thumb. "If you could go anywhere in the world right now, where would you go?"

Parker turned to face her, the random question pulling at his mind in a way he hadn't expected it to. It wasn't a hard question, he could think of a million places he'd like to go and see, but sitting there in the car with her made it kind of impossible to think of one place he'd rather be.

"I don't know. What about you?"

"I just want to see a palm tree."

Flashes of the vacations his so-called friends had brought him along on now dimmed the pure contentment he was feeling in her company. Guilt snuck in. He'd been gifted with things simply for being friends with the wrong people at the right time. He'd give anything to trade spaces with Summer for even just one of those trips.

He couldn't stop himself from kissing her. "Palm trees are nice."

She hummed thoughtfully as she settled into him again, quiet contentment descending upon them as they watched the rest of the movie.

The ride home was full of easy conversation and frozen yogurt. With the windows down, the cool night air whipped her air about, filling the car with the scent of her shampoo, which was now officially one of his favorite smells in the world.

Coming to a stop at a stop light, Summer snapped his picture, blinding him for a second with the flash.

"Easy on the eyes!"

She waved the picture back and forth before setting it aside with the others they'd taken. "I'm collecting memories over here."

"I see." He licked his lips thoughtfully as he slowly accelerated once again. Another idea began to form as they drove along the quiet streets. "How about we make one more?"

"What do you mean?"

Parker didn't answer her right away, he drove through two more intersections before things aligned in his favor. As the light in front of him turned red, he quickly threw the car into park and unbuckled his seatbelt while opening the door.

"Parker Reeves, what are you doing?!"

Instead of answering, he took off running a full lap around the car sliding into the driver's seat just as the light turned red again. One look at her flabbergasted and he could tell she had no idea what had just gone on.

"Fire drill." He supplied with a happy shrug. "Next light, it's your turn."

"I don't even know what to do!"

"It's really not complicated. Just run around the car and be back in your seat before the light turns green."

Summer gave him a single determined nod as she set the camera aside. She gathered her hair together in one hand and in some quick trick of the hand, tied it up in one of her bun thing-a-ma-bobs. "Let's do this thing."

Watching Summer run around the car, laughing and whooping in excitement was the best thing to come out of such a silly game. He snapped shots of her dancing around the car before joining her for a lap.

"That was fun."

Her cheeks were flushed as she sat next to him once again, her chest heaving in the aftermath of the both the running and laughing fits. Parker parked the car in his driveway and shut off the engine. He'd have to remember to thank Luke again.

"I'm glad you had fun." He glanced over at the empty driveway next to her house. "Your mom is gone?"

She nodded as she pulled her keys out of her purse. "She's on a new rotation for another few weeks. It's an overnight shift."

"Oh okay. Well let me walk you to your door and make sure you get in safely."

They collected their things from the car before they

headed in the direction of her front door, walking hand in hand. A cool breeze gusted just then, Summer shivering instinctively. The early setting of the sun and coolness of the night all pointed to the end of summer approaching. He wasn't ready for it to end.

"Thank you for a lovely evening, Mr. Reeves."

They came to a stop on her bottom step, flirtatiously dancing around what Parker hoped to God would be a good night kiss. He rubbed his thumb over the ring on her finger, just feeling its presence gave reinforcement to his feelings.

She pressed those perfectly pink lips of hers together, rolling them together as she contemplated what she was about to say next. He licked his lips in anticipation.

"Hey Parker... do you want to come in?"

The question was laced with desire and everything in his body reacted. He craved this girl something serious. His hormones screamed against his self-restraint. "I want to. But I don't know if that's the best idea right now. Maybe we should take some to time to think on it."

He almost couldn't believe the words that were coming out of his mouth. *Who was he?* He was a guy that was stupid in love.

"I have thought about it. To be honest, I haven't stopped thinking about it since the day I walked into your bedroom as you were trying to get dressed."

Her cheeks flushed pink as her eyes dropped from his face to his torso, and then back again. She looked him in the eyes when she asked him for the second time.

"Will you please come in?"

chapter Twenty Three

If he had to imagine what Summer's room would look like, he would have conjured up something very similar to this. Soft colors perfectly contrasted with bold colors filling the space with the very essence of who she was. Paper lanterns that hung from the ceiling cast a warm light over the room. His attention was drawn to the large bed.

It looked so inviting.

He had to think about something else... anything else.

Summer dropped her purse next to the door before kicking off her sneakers. "You can sit and get comfortable. I'm going to step out and call my mom to let her know we made it back safely."

Parker nodded and she left him alone.

He blew out a nervous breath, wringing his hands together. He didn't know if he could do this. He wanted to, God, did he want to. But the thought of actually going through with it gave him pause.

His hesitation had less to do about the 'what' and everything to do with the 'who' it would involve.

He'd been young and dumb before, but being young and in love, well that was new. He was determined not to screw this up. Parker had to make sure Summer knew she didn't have to do anything to keep him. She was the most important person in the world to him and taking care of her was his new priority. No matter what he wanted, wanting to respect her would always come first.

When she returned to the room, her face had been freshly washed and her hair was loosed from her bun and fell over her shoulders. She smiled softly at him. "You didn't get comfortable."

"About that..." Parker swallowed hard. His sentiments hadn't changed but with her standing in front of him, things started go fuzzy. He tried to remember the speech he had prepped in his head but when she pulled the top of her dress down revealing another lacy bra, he had forgotten his own name. His brain was officially short circuiting.

This girl...

He willed his eyes to move and his hands to stay still as he tried to pull his eyes away from her body so he could focus on her face. "I love you Summer, I want to respect you."

"I want to respect you too." She pushed herself up on the tips of her toes and planted a kiss along his jawline, peppering them down the side of his neck until she leaned into him. Her lips grazed the lobe of his ear as she smiled against it. "Take your shirt off and kiss me."

"So bossy... I had a dream about you that felt just like this, you know?"

Summer giggled as she took his shirt and tossed it to the side. Her hands were on him then, gripping his sides as she slowly walked backward in the direction of the bed. Feet tangling and fumbles slowed their movements until Parker scooped her up and carried her to the bed. Keeping her in his arms as he sat. Their kiss heated quickly and as she tugged at his waistband purposefully.

"I wanted to do this right. You know make it romantic, light a candle..." He spoke against her lips, not wanting to stop kissing her.

"We're seventeen. An empty house *is* romantic." She tucked her hair behind her ear. "I love the fact that you want to make me feel special, Parker, I really do. But I don't need that. I need you. I want you."

"I want you too." He grazed the soft skin of her sides. Placing kisses along her neck and chest as he moved to shift her beneath him. He groaned in complaint. "I don't have anything..."

"Remember the whole mom being a nurse thing? Check the drawer. Those suddenly appeared after she caught us the other day."

Parker didn't know whether to be grateful or embarrassed. He settled on the former as Summer threw her dress on the floor.

Parker lay next to her, his hand on her chest as he watched it rise and fall as she came back to earth. Just watching her was enough to get him going all over again. She looked blissfully satiated, Parker gave his ego a fist bump.

This was one memory he didn't need a picture to help

capture the details to remember later. He would never forget.

"Your heart is racing. Are you okay?"

Summer rolled over to face him pressing her lips to his bare chest to calm his concern before she tipped her back to look him in the eye. "My heart is racing because I'm so very much okay. I'm perfect. That was perfect."

He couldn't argue.

He had felt a connection with her he thought he was incapable of feeling. On an emotional level it was there, and on a physical level it led to fireworks. His skin still tingled from holding her so intimately.

She snuggled into his side, humming contentedly. Her eye lids were already closing as sleep came fast. "Thanks for the best date ever."

"You're welcome, sweetheart. Now close your eyes and get some rest. I'm not going anywhere."

Chapter Twenty Four

It was a sound breaking through the quiet still night air that jolted him out of his sleep. Trying to get his bearings straight, Parker rubbed the sleep out of his eyes. The sweet scent of Summer brought his memories into focus. Parker sat up suddenly, instantly aware and startled by her absence.

"Summer?"

No answer came as he scurried out of bed and grabbed his jeans from the floor. Quickly shoving his legs into them as he scurried out of the room and into the still dark hallway. He couldn't explain the feeling he got as he hurried to the steps, but there was only one that came to mind as he froze at the landing, fear.

Summer lay crumpled at the bottom of the steps. Her hair was spread about the crown of her head like a halo. His blood ran cold. He didn't think his feet touched the steps as he flew down to her side.

"Summer?!"

Her chest rose and fell rapidly as she struggled to catch a breath. Panic rose in his chest. He'd looked at over a hundred websites and videos since she had disclosed her condition and now he couldn't remember anything except that his girl was hurting. He brushed the hair off her forehead, placing a desperate kiss. A sob choked his words, "Hang in there sweetheart, I'm going to get a phone and get help."

He darted to the kitchen, grabbing the phone from the counter. He had already dialed 911 as he sprinted back to her side. He tried to keep his wits about him as he relayed whatever information the operator asked him for. With the reassurance that help was on the way, Parker left her side one more time as he took the stairs three at a time and burst back into her room where he collected their cell phones and his shirt from the floor.

Tapping out an urgent message to Luke on his phone, he charged back downstairs to Summer's side where he sat Summer upright and slid his shirt over her body. Something about preserving her privacy at this moment felt important even if it was irrelevant.

He unlocked her phone, he had to call Kelly. With Summer struggling to breathe, he needed to talk to someone who could tell him if he was doing something wrong. He couldn't screw this up.

Still listening for sirens, he felt the tiniest bit of relief when Kelly's voice came through the line after the second ring. "Hey hun, can't sleep?"

"Kelly! Something is wrong with Summer. She's sick..." The words felt rough on his throat. Brash but necessary. "The ambulance is on the way but I don't know what to do. I don't know how to help!"

Kelly's breath seized. "Parker, I need you to stay calm and tell me exactly what's going on."

Parker did his best to keep his voice steady as he relayed exactly how he had found her and her state while Summer squeezed his hand. He squeezed his eyes shut. He hadn't said a prayer since the day his mother stopped insisting he do so, but now he sat there hoping God still remembered his name.

"Parker, you did the right thing. I won't make it home before the ambulance gets there so I'll meet you here."

Any parting words and instructions were lost as the sound of ambulance arriving shattered any remaining quiet of the neighborhood. Parker scooped Summer up into his arms, cradling her to his chest as he hurried out of the door.

Luke was racing across the yard just as the paramedics threw the doors open. It was probably the first time all summer Parker actually felt relieved to see his father. He waved Parker on. "Go! I'll lock up their house and meet you there."

The ambulance ride was frenzied. Summer's eyes had finally closed as they covered her nose and mouth with a breathing mask, the medic assuring him it would help her get the oxygen she was in desperate need of. Terms like low saturation and EKGs were tossed over his head and questions were thrown his way, some of which he had the answer to but most were either lost in a pool of ignorance or panic.

She had to be okay.

She was going to be okay.

At the hospital, things began to move even faster as he

stepped back, letting Kelly rush alongside the gurney as they tried to get Summer the assistance she desperately needed. He was barely aware of the fact that he was now barefoot and bare chested, only wanting someone to come and tell him she was going to be okay. Better yet, he wanted to wake up from this nightmare.

Luke rushed towards him, putting his hands on either side of his shoulders. "Parker!"

"She's with Kelly. They're working on her."

Luke nodded, worry and trepidation still written all over his face. Parker took in his dad's sleep tousled hair and pajama pants paired with a cardigan and loafers. It was the look of someone who had dropped everything to show up when he was needed.

"I grabbed you some things. I know you ran out of the house... I thought you might like them."

Only then did Parker notice the plastic bag Luke held in his hand. He gratefully took it over to the nearest seat in the waiting room. He quickly pulled the shirt over his head, while simultaneously wiggled his feet into the untied Converse sneakers. "Thanks for bringing this stuff... and for coming."

Luke's eyes softened as he took the seat next to him. "Of course."

Parker wrung his hands together. "She's going to be alright."

It felt like an eternity had passed when Kelly appeared once again. Her face was calmer even if it looked like she had aged over the last couple of hours. Taking the seat next to him, she took hold of his hand and patted it lovingly.

"How are you holding up, Parker?"

It didn't matter how he felt. He shook his head. "How is she?"

"She's stable. They gave her some medications to deal with these effects and she should be breathing much better tomorrow. We're waiting on the results from some tests she took."

"It's all my fault."

"No, honey, it's not. Summer was born-"

Shaking his head he stood and faced her. "I know all that. I'm talking about tonight. You didn't want her to go to New York at first and I took her anyway. I kept her out all day. And then tonight... we... slept together. "

"Still not your fault. I promise you. You give Summer things I could never figure out how to give her, you give her something I spent her whole life wondering if she'd ever get a chance to experience how good it can be."

Parker wrapped her in a hug that she earnestly accepted. They stood like that for a long time. Holding each other in an understanding that they were probably talking to the only other person in the world to fully grasp the fear they felt.

"Can I see her?"

"Of course."

Luke assured Parker he would be fine in the waiting room while he went with Kelly, whose uniform got him past some hospital regulation about immediate family visiting only. Her private room was quiet save for the beeping of the machines monitoring the status of her heart. Someone had gathered her hair up into a messy bun and helped to dress her in a hospital gown. For the first time since he had met her, Summer looked exhausted. The oxygen mask had been removed, in its place was now a cannula.

He claimed a spot next to her beside her bed and kissed her lips softly, relishing the small bit of peace that came over him as he did so.

"Hey, how are you feeling?"

A shadow of a smile flickered. "Tired."

"I bet." He gently traced his thumb alongside the side of her jaw. "Your mom snuck me back here so I could see you really quick but I want you to try and rest up as much as you can, sweetheart. I'm going to be back in a couple of hours."

"Mm. 'Kay." She took a breath, and it was the sweetest sound he'd ever heard. "Love you, Parker."

"I love you so much, Summer."

Chapter Twenty Five

Sleep eluded him.

Parker lay in bed staring at the stupid popcorn ceiling and remembering how quickly things had gone from perfect to terrifying. He turned the past few days over and over in his mind, dissecting every little detail searching for clues he might have missed. He had to have missed something. His gut churned with guilt. Knowing Summer wasn't sleeping soundly just next door filled him with an ache that thoroughly unsettled him with a need to see her.

Shadows danced along the wall until disappearing with the sun's arrival over the horizon. Parker got out of bed, shoving his body into action. After a hot shower and fresh change of clothes, he felt his mind set grow more positive. He sat in the kitchen and prepared himself a bowl of cereal. He stared at the clock as he chewed bite after bite, tasting nothing.

Unwilling to wait another minute, Parker grabbed his phone and wallet and headed to the garage to get his bike. He had to get to the hospital as soon as visiting hours were in effect. Going to pull the garage door open, Parker stopped short to see a note from his father telling him to use the car to get back to the hospital.

For the second time in twenty-four hours, a flash of gratitude for Luke popped up again in his heart.

Hospitals had always weirded him out. He couldn't think of them without thinking about sickness and mortality. No teenager wanted to walk into a place and remind themselves of where they could end up. But Summer had walked into one on more than one occasion and had her life saved. For that reason, he was grateful to walk into the doors of this one.

Getting directions to her new recovery room, Parker walked along the corridor thinking about how many times Summer had walked the same route, wondering how many times she checked in without knowing if or when she'd be able to check out. The reality check was profound.

When Parker stepped into Summer's hospital room, he was pleasantly surprised to see Summer sitting up in bed, cannula still in place as she sat with her legs crossed frowning at the television. Various machines stood nearby monitoring her heart in so many different ways he couldn't keep track. But he couldn't focus on any of that right now. Everything he had inside was focused on her. His chest relaxed with the first deep breath taken in hours. Seeing her reminded him how to breathe.

"Well you look really happy to see me."

She rolled her eyes, a full smile on her lips. "I would be happier if you had a short stack of pancakes in your hands."

"Ah, I knew I left something in the car." He snapped his fingers as he delivered his quip. He crossed the plain white tile floors to deliver the kiss he was aching to give her. It was soft and quick, but it was real. He needed to feel real after last night.

"So have I completely scared you away?" Summer asked him as he took a seat at the edge of her bed. "I mean I'm probably the only girl who loses her virginity and has a cardiac event in the same night."

Parker cocked his head to the side. "I'm here, aren't I?"

She gave his hand a squeeze, looking displeased at her now bare ring finger. "I can't wear my ring while I'm in here."

He shook off the unnecessary explanation. "Didn't you promise me that you would tell me if you weren't feeling well, Summer? We could have taken it easier, I wouldn't have pushed you so much..."

"Stop, Parker. That's not how any of this works." She pulled her hand away from him then. He could tell he was riding the fine line that divided her patience and her annoyance. It was a conversation he wanted to have, one they needed to have, but one that could also wait until things had calmed down with her health. He didn't need to set her off with an argument.

"So, what did the doctor say?"

On cue, the door opened announcing the return of Kelly along with another woman. The royal blue scrubs she wore under her white coat gave her status away. This had to be Summer's cardiologist. She had creamy brown skin, her hair pulled into a neat bun at the nape of her neck, Parker focused in on her smile. It was a good smile, kind and sincere. He liked the look of that smile.

"Dr. York, this is Parker..." As Kelly's words faltered for

a second, Parker's gaze fell on her. She looked tired, which was understandable, but her eyes... there was something else there. Fear, exhaustion, sadness. It troubled something deep within him. He stood moving to stand beside the head of the bed.

"My boyfriend." Summer clarified. "Parker is my boyfriend. Parker, this is Dr. York. She's my cardiologist and a total rock star. Check out her kicks."

Hearing her call him her boyfriend out loud and in front of people, gave him goosebumps. He liked that title more than he ever had. Belonging to Summer felt like where he was always supposed to be.

Dr. York pushed her hands in her pockets and rocked on the balls of her feet. A pair of bright purple Converse on her feet. Parker gave Summer a pointed grin.

"It's nice to meet you." They exchanged a handshake and smile.

Kelly sniffed. "Dr. York wanted to talk to us about the test results."

"Okay. Go ahead."

Parker took a step towards the door before Summer's hand shot out to stop him. "You can stay."

She gave a pointed look to both women. "He can stay. I want him to stay."

Kelly looked at them both before giving Dr. York the go ahead nod of the head. It was then that Parker saw the change in the doctor's smile. It had gone from kind to sympathetic.

"Summer..."

Summer instantly began nodding her head. Her lips

pressed together as she turned to him. "This is going to be an 'I've got bad news and I've got worse news' situation. You might want to grab a chair."

Kelly sniffed. Parker sat. Summer cleared her throat.

"So, break it to me, Dr. York. How bad is it?"

"It's not good." The doctor came closer to Summer's bed adjusting the stethoscope around her neck. The smile had now completely vanished and a thin stressed line had taken its place. He had the startling feeling that this was going to be way worse than bad. "We've known that things could take a turn like this for a while. But I don't think any of us planned on it turning this hard and this fast. I've started the necessary steps to get you placed on the list..."

It was Summer's turn to sniff now, blinking back anything that would show how she felt. Parker gripped the arm rests of the chair, using every bit of energy he had not to erupt. Long syllabled words that meant something very bad for his girl began to swim in his head, getting all jumbled up with this nightmarish feeling churning deep in his gut. His own heart ached with every pump. He felt like he was betraying her, just sitting there all healthy while she had to hear the list of everything that was wrong.

"The left side of your heart..."

He couldn't hear anything. It felt like white noise. A high-pitched ringing in his ears. He wondered if this is what it felt like to have a brain aneurysm. It was as if his brain was trying to protect himself from what he was hearing. He couldn't process anything going wrong with her. This was *his* Summer.

Dr. York's voice pulled him back from the edge. "Even this will only be a temporary solution until we get you a new heart. We're pretty much out of options."

"I'm tired of running, Mom. How many times are we going to do this, huh? How many times are they going to cut me open and sew me up and pray it holds for another couple of years? How many times are you all going to tell me this surgery is going to be 'the great one'? Now I have to wait around hoping for someone to die so I can live!"

"Summer, calm down, please." Kelly swooped in cradling her daughter's face in between her hands.

"I'm so freaking tired, Mom."

Kelly lovingly kissed her daughter's forehead, "I know, baby. But maybe you could think about this, Dr. York thinks that it's your only option to keep you stable while waiting."

Summer pushed her away. Turning on her side she pulled the blankets over her head. "I want to be alone."

No one moved right away. Parker didn't know about them, but he was afraid if he made a move, if he blinked for just a second too long, she would be gone.

"Go. Away!"

They did listen then. Silent shuffling out of the room followed. Kelly grabbed a fresh Kleenex from her pocket and dabbed at her eyes. Parker knew he should comfort her, he wanted to. But he couldn't. His heart was breaking in his chest and he couldn't do a thing about it because the only thing that could fix it was in the other room demanding to be left alone.

"I don't know what to do. I've never seen her like this." Kelly quietly lamented.

Dr. York gave her hand a tender squeeze. "As a doctor, I know this is her only option. She won't make it more than a month on the transplant list if we don't intervene. But as a mom, as someone who has known that girl since her very first surgery, I get it. I know how much she's been through. Give her a day. She's stable, we'll keep her monitored."

Parker took a step backwards. And then another. He did that until he was running out of the hospital and down the street. Forgetting all about the car in the parking lot, Parker's legs pumped harder and faster until he was running full speed through town.

Words he never wanted to hear replayed on a loop in his head, driving him hard and faster until he burst through the front door of his house. His chest was heaving with pure anger and anguish as he nearly took his bedroom door off the hinge as he tried to go back to where his summer began, he wanted a do-over; he wanted time. His heart was beating too loud, too fast; a constant reminder of the thing threatening his happiness.

He screamed.

He screamed loud and long. He tried to infuse each vibration of his vocal cords with pain. Feeling no relief, he did it again and again until the sob broke through his war cry on the world. His hand burst the glass of his bedroom window. Blood instantly began to flow and dripped from his fingertips as he collapsed to the floor.

"Parker! What's going on?! Oh my God, Parker-"

Luke's voice came from behind him, and then from beside him. For the first time in fifteen years, Parker felt his dad's arms embrace him.

"Dad..."

Chapter Twenty Six

Parker checked out his bandaged hand. It had taken a taxi ride and a dozen stitches to get his hand cleaned up. Luke stood next to him in a blood-stained shirt, as they came to a stop in front of the car he'd left behind earlier that day.

"Sorry about the window. I'll get a job and pay for it."

"I'm not worried about the window, Parker." His father's hand cupped his shoulder. "After you and your mom left, I took a few panes of glass out myself."

"You?!" Parker couldn't see his father ever getting upset about anything beyond students handing in their assignments late, but if this summer with Luke had taught him anything it was that maybe he'd never really known his father.

Luke looked humorously indignant. "Don't look so surprised!"

The two stood quiet for moment. Luke's gaze drifting back over to the main entrance of the hospital. "You sure you don't want to go see her?"

"Going to see her is not my problem, it's knowing what to say to her is where I'm struggling. I want to scream, cry, and kiss her all at the same time. I want to go rip a heart out of someone's chest right now for her and I'm sure it means I'm absolutely out of my mind but I don't care because I freaking love that girl in there. And she's dying…"

"She's still here and there's still hope. There's always hope." Luke pulled him into another embrace.

It wasn't awkward or unwanted. It felt something like home.

"Want to grab a bite? You should probably eat something with those pain meds they gave you."

Parker shrugged and reluctantly agreed. He hadn't eaten since his flavorless bowl of cereal that morning but his appetite was completely shot.

Luke stopped and picked up their food order on the drive back to the house and less than an hour later they were sitting at the dining room table almost as if they were an honest to God family.

"I knew about everything she'd been through with her heart. I knew where things stood, at least I thought I did. I walked into the hospital today just wanting her to feel better and I walked out knowing every odd is stacked against her. I'm mad, I'm sad… I'm feeling everything right now."

He clenched his hand, wincing as the flare of pain reminded him of his last angry outburst. He relaxed his hand placing the bag of frozen vegetables back over his bandage. Summer was going to tear him a new one over this.

"So, what are you going to do?"

Parker pushed his food around his plate with the back of his fork. He'd only managed a couple of bites before the flavors began to resemble sawdust in his mouth. The thought of eating another bite turned his stomach. He dropped his fork to his plate. "I'm only seventeen, I'm not even out of high school yet..."

He thought about the first time he laid eyes on Summer. How she stood with that rusted bicycle tire willing to risk tetanus to check something off a list. Her bucket list. God, the once silly words now soured in his mouth.

She had done nearly everything she had set out to do that summer.

It was his turn to show the same fortitude. He looked Luke in the eyes. "But I love that girl. I'm not going anywhere."

"You're a good man, better than most." Luke placed a loving hand on his shoulder. "C'mon, I want to show you something."

Parker followed his father as they moved upstairs. He hadn't bothered much with this floor of the house since he arrived. Much like the rest of the house, things had felt very much frozen in time. Memories rolled through quickly as he walked along the creaky wood floors.

"I know you said you weren't interested but I went ahead and did a little early fall cleaning." Luke turned the knob of one of closed bedroom doors. Opening it, he ushered Parker past him into the space. The walls had been freshly painted. A larger air mattress sat in the middle of the room and dresser sat against the wall.

He had no idea when Luke had done any of this. Then again, spending every possible minute with Summer and trying his best to avoid Luke could explain that.

"I won't be able to have the window replaced until early next week so I thought you might like to start sleeping in here. Make the room your own. I can order some furniture and get a real bed in here, so if you decide you want to visit again... I'm not going anywhere either, Parker."

He nodded. Any words he did have catching in his throat.

"Well I'll leave you to it. I'm going to go put away the food."

He didn't answer as Luke left him alone in the quiet of the room. Taking a seat on the edge of the mattress he peered out of the window his gaze locked onto Summer's dark bedroom window. He pulled out his phone and quickly typed out a text message to her.

Parker: I'm here and I'm not going anywhere. I'll see you in the morning.

Parker: I love you

Three dots teased him with her reply. He brought his uninjured hand to his mouth as he waited for her answer.

Summer: I love you too. Come at 10:00. I'm calling a meeting.

Parker: I'll be there at 9:59 boss

He rapped three times on the semi-open hospital room door. He shifted the Styrofoam container he held gingerly in his injured hand as he stepped into the room.

"Summer, are you decent?"

He heard her snort in laughter just beyond the partially pulled hospital curtain. He couldn't blame her. The question felt all wrong in his mouth, like somewhere some wildly mature middle age man had taken up residence in his brain.

"Hey."

The weight of his feelings for her sat in his chest so heavily he practically breathed the word. Her cheeks held a little more color today, which despite the doctor's prognosis, he decided to take as a phenomenal sign.

"You look beautiful sweetheart."

"You're really cute when you lie." She gave him a gentle smile, extending her hand out to him. "Come and sit with me. I want to talk to you before everyone else comes in."

"What's in the box?"

He grinned. "I picked up an order of pancakes from the diner for you."

"Aw, you really do love me!"

She beamed as he sat the container on the bedside table and took her hand as he sat on the edge of the bed. Before she could speak, he cupped her cheek in his hand. Their lips met. A kiss full of fear and need; want and uncertainty. But mainly there was love.

Her soft hands held onto his face. "Sorry I yelled at you yesterday."

"Are you kidding me? You deserved to yell, to be angry, and to cry. Don't apologize for feeling. Not with me." He kissed her again. This time it was full of reassurance and comfort. They both needed that kiss.

She smiled, dropping her gaze to his hurt hand. "What happened?!"

"It's nothing, I'm fine."

Ignoring his nonchalance, she cradled his hand in her lap like she wasn't the one with something far more serious going on. He didn't care what they said, the heart this girl had was amazing.

"Tell me the truth, Parker Reeves."

"I had an incident with a window yesterday. Luke took me to get all stitched up, I'll be fine in a week or two, I promise."

A look of complete understanding passed over her face. She pressed a kiss to his hand.

"So, about what was laid out yesterday, I know it was a lot of information all at once and I'm sure it got weird and technical."

"I got the gist of it."

She nodded. "I know you didn't sign up for any of this." She gestured wildly around the room.

"I signed up for you. I love you, and I'm gonna be here for you. You're the kind of girl I can love forever."

She closed her eyes, sighing sadly. "I might not have forever in me, Parker."

"Then I'll take as long as you've got."

They embraced and Parker closed his eyes too. If he concentrated solely on the way she felt in his arms or if he relished the way his lips still tingled from their kiss, then maybe he could imagine them away to somewhere where they could just be. Somewhere with palm trees.

Another knock came then followed by a small parade of bodies. Along with Kelly, Dr. York arrived with two other white coats this time. He didn't pay attention to their names because his brain could only focus on what was about to come out of Summer's mouth next.

"Dearly beloved, we're gathered here today..."

Summer snorted at her own joke which caused Parker to snicker. The adults in the room either sat oblivious to the joke or bewildered about the idea of a sense of humor.

"First, I'd like it put on record that I stand by my original statement about being fed up with surgeries and being sick."

Dr. York nodded with a small smile. "Noted."

"Good. I've decided we can move forward with using the LVAD as a bridge to a transplant."

Kelly folded her palms together, her lips pressed into a thin line because she, like Parker, knew there was a 'but' coming."

"But the surgery has to be done next week."

Mouths opened in objection all around the room, Parker's included. Summer, like the boss she was, powered on.

"I want a week. I want a week out of this hospital before I go through surgery and recovery again."

Her doctor stepped forward. "Summer, we barely have been able to get you stable. The sooner we do this the better…"

"I need one week. I want to go home, please."

He didn't know about the rest of them but the earnest plea grabbed him by the heart. He would do anything for this girl, but he had no idea what they would say. He gave her a reassuring kiss on the forehead.

chapter Twenty Seven

After a million and two stipulations, Summer had actually did it. She was coming home. Parker was excited for her to be in the comfort of her own space even if he was wary about the risk she was taking. But when he remembered she was the only one who had to live in her body, he reminded himself she had spent her life learning and living within her limits. He had to trust her the same way he had asked her to trust him.

He also had a promise to keep. He told her he would help her have a great summer and this week was going to be no exception, even if he had to get creative and keep her relaxed and stress free.

When Kelly's car pulled up to the driveway, Parker was waiting on the front porch like the love-sick puppy of a boyfriend he was. He jogged over to the car, pulling open the passenger side door before Kelly had even turned the ignition off. Summer's shoulder's shook with her gentle laughter, as she gave him her hand to help her out.

"Can you help her inside, Parker? I'm going to unload

the oxygen tank."

"I'm capable of walking to the front door- "

Parker didn't let her finish the sentence, instead sweeping her off her feet and carrying her into the house. Capable or not, it gave him a fantastic excuse to get his hands on her.

"Careful there, I'm pretty sure swooning is on the list of things I'm not allowed to do for the next week. It's somewhere between sex and tap dancing."

"What about teasing your boyfriend? I asked them to add that one in specifically."

Placing her on her feet, he lovingly hugged her. "Welcome home. I missed you."

"Have you been reviewing the SAT stuff I sent over to you?"

He put the game controller down and tried his best not to look completely dumbfounded. He'd been a little preoccupied this week to say the least. Now that he had her for a few short days before a major surgery, a test was the last thing on his mental agenda. They had been relaxing for most of the day, with Kelly popping in periodically to check on her, Summer seemed at ease. As she rested comfortably on the couch, he brought over his game system and they'd spent time cuddling and gaming, which was a surprisingly amazing replacement for Netflix and chilling.

"I think I'm going to reschedule it."

"No."

That was her reply, just a flat no. As if he was the one

being crazy right now.

"What do you mean, no?"

"You're going to take the test in two days. You're ready for it, Parker. You don't get to postpone your future because of me."

You are my future. The words hung heavily on the tip of his tongue. He would tell her, just not now. He exhaled. "Okay, I'll take it."

"Good. Now hand over the controller and let me show those boys how it's done."

"Will you come straight over when you come back from testing?"

He looked up at her from where he lay his head in her lap. They'd spent the rainy afternoon posting pictures on her board and reading books in the quiet privacy of her shed. Before this summer, he had never been the type to actively enjoy the state of just being. It was nice.

"Where else would I go?"

She ignored his sarcasm. "Will you?"

There was something else in her eyes. Something that went deeper below any surface question about seeing him after a test. It disquieted his own inner peace. Taking her hand, he kissed her palm.

"Of course I will. You're the only one I ever want to see."

Pressing his hand to her cheek she looked down at him. He felt like he would drown in the sadness filling her eyes. Closing her eyes, she took a breath.

"I can't believe there's only five days left."

Parker shook his head. "Don't think like that. There's five more days we can spend together, five more days for you to keep me in line, and five more days I can kiss you."

She chuckled lightly. "Five more days for you to read to me?"

"I can do that."

Parker rolled off her lap towards the bookshelf. "I'm picking this time. Close your eyes."

Summer protested lightly before doing as he asked. When he was certain that her eyes were sufficiently closed, he pulled the worn paperback off the shelf before coming to sit at her side.

Clearing his throat dramatically, he turned to the front page and began reading, "Where's Papa going with that ax?"

The opening line of *Charlotte's Web* caused her eyes to pop open with a special smile. "I knew you were going to pick that one!"

"It's a good one. It makes me think of you."

She nestled in to him, pulling the thin crocheted blanket around her shoulders and resting her head on his shoulder. "Because it's my favorite?"

"At first that was the reason. Now I know it's because it reminds me of the two of us."

"Huh, how so? And you better not be trying to call me a pig!" She nudged him in the ribs.

"Oh, I'm definitely the pig." Parker twisted his mouth in thought, sorting through the words in his head to make sure they came out right. "Charlotte saved Wilbur's life. When no one else could see Wilbur for anything but what they wanted to see him as, Charlotte did. She became his friend and made him look good to everyone else…"

Parker paused, fearing the next few words he spoke had the potential to make him look lame or worse yet stupid. "You're my Charlotte, Summer. I wouldn't have gotten through this summer without you. You've turned my life around, sweetheart. You saved me from my own self destruction."

Summer lifted her head, meeting his eyes. The moment didn't need words or explanation. She understood. She always understood.

She kissed him softly, letting her love linger on his lips for as long as she could.

"Keep reading."

Chapter Twenty Eight

It was way too early for this much work.

That was the thought running through his mind on a constant loop.

When Parker showed up to the testing site at 7:52 in the morning, he was about 99.9999% sure everything about this decision was wrong. For starters, when Luke dropped him off that morning he was reminded he'd be better off leaving his cell phone in the car because for the next three hours and some change he was officially cut off from technology. Then, he was sat in a room where he listened to a list of dos and don'ts before he even broke the seal of the test.

Instructed to begin, Parker froze. The idea of just quitting again crossed his mind. He'd get an easy six hundred points just for sitting there zombied out. He was sitting there staring at the pencil in his hand wondering if he could do it, when he finally asked himself what he was so afraid of.

He knew the answer.

It was the same thing Summer saw in him from the moment she heard about him getting ready to piss away the rest of his academic future and, in turn, his life as a mere point in his emotional vendetta plot. If the test went ahead and put a number to his true potential, then he could no longer hide behind the pretense he'd spent years crafting. It had never been about whether he could do the work, it was always about his drive. He'd have to take everything he did this summer and make it happen. The old Parker would have put his head down on the desk and slept for the next three and a half hours. Being real, not only would the old Parker not have showed up, he wouldn't even have registered.

But he did and he was here. It was time to cross something off a list that had intimidated him for far too long. Parker picked up his ordinary yellow pencil and went to work.

When he stepped out into the sunlight again after several hours of fluorescent lighting, bubbling in multiple choice answers and working his way through an insane number of math problems, Parker felt free. He stretched his arms above his head, rolling his neck from side to side as he walked towards the parking lot where Luke had told him he'd be waiting for him. Since he also felt hungry he was relieved to see his father's Subaru parked under a shady elm tree.

Happiness flooded his veins when he spotted Summer's red hair sitting in the passenger seat. He should have known she'd find a way to make sure she'd be the first person he saw after the testing. Picking up his pace, he jogged over to the car as quietly as he could, he leaned through the open window and surprised her with a kiss to her neck.

When she turned to face him revealing her oxygen cannula, a thorn of concern pierced his excitement. Her saturation levels had improved in the hospital and had remained stable for the past few days so while she had to take things easy, she had been able to go without the extra assistance.

Cupping her face in his hands, his thumbs gingerly traced the thin tube. "How are you feeling?"

"I'm okay. Just a precaution."

Her two simple words spoke volumes more than most people could probably ever comprehend.

"I thought Summer would like to take the ride here to pick you up."

Luke's voice reminded him they weren't alone. Parker nodded his appreciation to Luke before opening the door to help Summer out. At the sight of her wearing his t-shirt, the one he hurriedly covered her in as they rushed to the hospital on the night after her birthday, his heart skipped a beat. With their noticeable difference in size, his shirt would have normally dwarfed her petite frame, but through the magic of a very well placed knot, and pairing it with some denim shorts and sunshine yellow Converse sneakers, she was adorable, cute, and sexy all in one perfect package.

"You look good in my clothes."

She hugged him, bringing his ear near her lips and whispered, "You look good out of your clothes."

His heart didn't just skip then. It threatened to tumble, somersault, and cartwheel out of his chest. *This girl.*

He gave her a loaded look as he reached back into the front seat, collecting the backpack that held her portable oxygen tank. He settled her into the back seat of the car before sliding in next to her. Her hand immediately found his as she looked at him and told him seven words he was sure he'd never forget.

I love you. I'm proud of you.

chapter Twenty nine

Luke was sipping from a mug of coffee when Parker yawned his way to the kitchen. Though he stayed up watching movies with Summer until she fell asleep, he felt like he'd finally had his first decent night's sleep since going to New York. Spotting Luke in his usual work outfit for the first time in a couple of days, he stopped short as he put his hand on the handle of the refrigerator.

"Going in to work?"

Luke nodded and sat his mug aside. "I have some meetings I have to be present at today. Departmental stuff that needs to be handled before the fall semester, you know?"

Parker shrugged. He knew enough he guessed. "I wanted to know if you were going to be home for dinner tonight, I wanted to invite Kelly and Summer over. They've done a lot for me the last few months I thought the least I could do was invite them over for dinner to say thanks."

"Oh, yeah, of course-"

Luke's stammering felt a lot like nervousness, though Parker had no idea what Luke would be nervous about. He was the one throwing himself on the sword here by going along with this plan of Summer's.

"Do you want me to pick something up from a restaurant? Or you could always order in, I can give you some money."

He shook his head. "I'm going to actually cook dinner for them."

He didn't know if it was possible for anyone to look as shocked as Luke did.

"I didn't know you could cook."

"I can't. So, it's probably going to be a disaster." Parker pulled the fridge open and pulled out a carton of juice before grabbing a glass from the cabinet.

"Well, how about you take the car today? You can drop me off on campus and take the car to get to the grocery store and everything. I can carpool it home."

"That'd help." He downed the cup of juice before placing it in the sink. "I'll go throw some clothes on and run over to check on Summer really quick. I can meet you at the car in fifteen?"

Parker vaguely heard his father's agreement before he was running back upstairs and pulling out clothes to throw on. Ninety seconds later and he was heading down the stairs again and out of the back door.

Parker knocked on the patio door before sliding it open and letting himself into Kelly and Summer's kitchen. Both were sitting at the small kitchen table eating a bowl of fruit salad, and greeted him with a smile and a warm good morning.

"Would you like to join us for breakfast? We have plenty."

"Thanks, but no thanks. I have to run a few errands this morning but I wanted to come by and invite you both over to dinner tonight."

Summer's eyes widened with elation. Her constant request was finally coming to fruition. The thought of setting their parents up still nauseated him, but he knew it would make her happy. With only three days left until her surgery, he wanted to make her happy as often as possible.

"That sounds lovely. What time should we be there?"

"Six thirty. My father will be joining us as well so..." Parker's warning faded away as Summer side eyed him.

"We'll be there."

Luke had been driving for about ten minutes when he suddenly turned down the radio and cleared his throat. Parker braced himself for the conversation he already knew was coming. It had been one he had anticipated having for a few days now because as slow as the first days of summer had crawled by, the last days were flying by.

"Have you talked to your mother? I told her about your taking the SATs, she was thrilled."

"I haven't talked to her so I wouldn't know."

Another clearing of the throat. "She called because it's about time to begin arranging your return to New York. School starts in a week and she was pretty concerned about you missing the first day."

The idea of leaving Concord didn't sit well with him at all. In less than seventy-two hours, Summer would be going into some operating room so being on time for homeroom was not on his list of things he needed to be worried about.

"And what if I don't want to go? Do I get a say this time?"

Luke's brow furrowed as he looked at Parker, taking his eyes off the road for several seconds longer than Parker felt comfortable with. "Of course you do."

"Then I'll stay here in Concord... with you. If that's alright?"

"Of course it is. I would love to have you stay, Parker. But I do think Laura needs to hear that from you."

He was right of course. Hurt as he felt, this decision had nothing to do with punishing her and the least he could do is call her and let her know what he wanted. "I'll call her this afternoon."

Parker sat on the wide wooden steps of the back porch, his gaze falling over to Summer's shed as he idly rubbed his thumb across the screen of his phone. After spending weeks of dodging his mother's calls, promising to call her was a lot easier said than done. She was going to be hurt it took him this long to pick up the phone and call, while he was still hurt that she hadn't noticed this new life she took him into had already chewed him up and spit him out. No matter how it was sliced, there was going to be a lot of hurt on both lines.

He pressed the small but important green button on the screen before bringing it up to his ear. Three rings was all it took before the familiar voice sounded in his ear.

"Parker?"

There was a twinge of something in his chest. "Yeah, Mom. It's me."

"I was prepared to give you a piece of my mind and ground you, but now I just feel relieved to hear your voice."

"Ground me? Can you do that when I'm living with someone else?"

"I'm your mother."

Her tone was light and the banter felt familiar. The easygoing nature of their relationship didn't feel so distant in the moment. It gave him a small bit of relief that he planned on using to carry him through the rest of the conversation.

"I guess I should have dangled the coming home carrot sooner to get you to answer a call."

"That's kind of why I'm calling," Parker cleared his throat. "I'm not coming back."

The silence on the line was so intense that if it wasn't for the sudden sound of a tense intake of air that came across the line, he would have thought she had hung up.

"If this is about you being mad about spending your summer with Luke-"

"It's not. Well it is, but not for the reason you think."

He heard his mother clear her throat tightly. He could imagine her standing in the middle of the expansive kitchen, her mouth twisted in displeasure at his declaration. "Okay, so tell me why."

Another glance at the shed felt like a nudge to his ribs from Summer. It was time to have a conversation that was long overdue. "I've been mad at you for a long time, Mom, even before this summer. When I got to Concord, it felt like the world was against me."

"Even me?"

"Especially you." Parker stood and walked down the steps into the yard where he began walking in slow laps. "When you met Charles, I feel like I fell off your radar. You were heading off to fancy dinner parties and charity galas, while I was struggling with feeling like neither of my parents wanted anything to do with me."

"Parker, that's not true-"

"It's how I felt, mom. You were the one who was always there for me, and when it felt like you weren't anymore, I guess I didn't know any other way to feel. After you got married and we moved out of Brooklyn, it got worse. I didn't even have my real friends anymore either."

Laura sniffed. "But you had Kroy and Trent."

"They were never my real friends."

For the first time in a long time, Parker talked to his mom. He told her the truth she never asked for and revealed Kroy and Trent's guilt in the scandal that had tarnished his reputation and threatened his future.

"You didn't tell me, Parker!"

Parker licked his lips before giving her one more honest answer. "You didn't ask me, Mom."

He heard another muffled sniffle but didn't let it halt his words. It felt good to let it out finally. "I'm not going to make any excuses for why I let my grades get as bad as they did but the whole thing didn't make me feel like trying anymore. I kinda just gave up on everyone, including myself. Until this summer…"

"Your dad has been telling me about all the stuff you've been doing. "

Parker chuckled. "Yeah, I finally put some energy into something other than feeling angry."

Laura's teary laughter joined his.

"I want to stay in Concord, not because I'm angry at you. I want to stay because for the first time in a long time, I feel like I'm home. I'm happy here."

"You can't be happy here?"

Parker paused. Standing still he looked up and realized he was almost in the exact spot as he was the first time he hopped the fence to talk to Summer. The memory caused his heart to flip flop in his chest.

"I don't think I can. You see, there's this girl..."

Parker went on to tell his mother about the girl who captured his eye, his interest, and his heart. With the exception of a few interjections of amusement or curiosity, she didn't interrupt his word frenzy as he tried to describe the force of nature Summer was.

Finally, he took a breath.

"Well I guess I'll start packing up your things for you. I'll call the school in the morning and discuss transferring your records over." Her voice was still sad but sounded resigned to the idea of his move.

He smiled to himself. "Thanks, Mom."

"Of course, I'll need to talk to your father."

Parker bit back a chuckle. Luke was going to be thrilled about that.

He checked the time on his phone. "Oh man, I'm running behind schedule. Mom, I need to go the grocery store. I'm trying to cook dinner tonight and I need to get some things."

"You? Cook?"

Parker could hear the shock waves all the way from

New York. "I said 'trying.'"

"Make spaghetti. It's kind of hard to screw it up."

He nodded. Another easy smile spread across his face. "I'll do that."

"I'll call you in a couple of days and we can arrange getting your things to you. And Parker? I miss you."

"I miss you too, Mom."

Parker used a wooden spoon to stir his spaghetti sauce. His mother's advice had paid off and the odds had worked in his favor as he pulled the spoon away from his lips quite pleased with both the sauce and himself. Checking the time on his phone, he quickly went to work trying his best to replicate the table at one of his mother's dinner parties. Setting the flowers he'd picked up in the only vase he could find in the house, he set them in the center of the now table cloth covered dining room table.

His guests would be arriving in just a few minutes because they were punctual people, unlike his father who had apologetically texted him no less than three times stating he was running late.

Apparently Parker was going to have to get used to it. Now that he was staying in Concord, he and Luke would have to get used to each other on a more permanent basis. It was strange how even that didn't send him running for the hills. A lot had changed in just a few short months.

Luke entered the garage door with two bouquets of flowers, just as the doorbell sounded announcing the arrival of Summer and Kelly.

Parker's eyes widened at the flowers in his father's hand. Apparently he did have a reason to be nervous.

Parker knew what it looked like when you had a crush on the red head beauty next door, and that look was all over Luke's face right about now.

Summer was going to jump all over this.

With their parents both thoroughly and surprisingly deep in conversation, Parker used the opportunity to pull Summer away from the table and into the kitchen where he could enjoy a private moment alone with her. He had only spent a brief moment with her that morning and it wasn't nearly enough to fill his beautiful girl quota for the day. She stood before him in her sundress and sneakers looking at him with her brilliant eyes filled to the brim with excitement.

"It looks like it's going well! What do you think?"

"I think I came in here to feel up my girlfriend, not talk about my dad giving my girlfriend's mother the eyes."

"He does have rather nice eyes." Summer teased him.

"What did I tell you about that?!" He pressed a kiss to her lips. "You know this just means that I have to marry you before my dad gets any ideas about making you my step-sister."

Summer's eyes filled up with love and went all soft as she gazed up at him. She placed her hands on his chest as he locked his arms around her lower back and held her near to him.

"I talked to my mom today."

Her eyebrows rose in eager curiosity. "How'd that go?"

"It went as good as it could have considering I've actively ignored her for months. Turns out she didn't like that. I also got to talk to her about the things I didn't like very much. She listened, though, and that makes me feel like maybe things will really get back to how it used to be between us."

"I'm happy for you."

"You know, the main reason I finally called her was because I had to let her know that I wasn't going to New York next week since I decided to stay here in Concord with Luke."

"And me?"

Parker nodded and kissed her again, this time more tenderly. "Of course you. And don't try and tell me that I have to leave you out of my decision. I love you, Summer… and not in some dumb summer fling type of way. When I have to make a plan for my future, you are always going to be a factor because you are my plans."

"I wasn't going to say that!"

He cocked his head to the side with a grin double dipped in disbelief. "Okay, so tell me what you were going to say."

She giggled. "You're not going to believe me now!"

"Try me."

She licked her lips and exhaled softly. "I was going to say that I love you too."

She was wrong. He absolutely believed her.

Chapter Thirty

When Parker walked into Summer's kitchen the next morning with only forty-eight hours left before surgery time, he had a plan and a proposition in mind for Kelly who greeted him with her usual welcoming smile. "Hey Parker, she's already out in her shed."

"I know, that's why I came here first. I was actually hoping to ask you for your permission, and your assistance."

"Well that sounds like something I guess we should sit for. Fortunately, I have some muffins for us to eat as well."

He nibbled his way through a blueberry muffin as he explained what he hoped to do in just a few short hours. Kelly's face remained stoic for much of the conversation, leading him to believe he had barked up the wrong tree. But then she smiled.

"I think that's an awesome idea, Parker."

He nearly choked on his muffin. "You do?"

"Yes. I really do. I think it will be a fun distraction for

her before everything." She chuckled, a heavy smile coming over her face. "You know, Summer and I, we've been dealing with her heart condition for a while. While the realistic part of my nurse brain always knew this could happen, all of my heart hoped it wouldn't. But I could have never expected you to come into her life and give her everything you've given her."

"I haven't done that much."

She grabbed his hand and squeezed it, giving him a firm shake of her head. "But you have. You love her, Parker. That's all I could have dreamed of for my daughter."

Parker swallowed. Accepting her praise was harder to do than it probably should have been. He'd spent so long absorbing other people's criticisms, it was sort of hard to believe he could do anything right. Proving he could do at least one thing right was a big deal. Proving that he could love Summer right? Well, that meant everything.

With Kelly on board, it was time for Parker to talk to Summer and see if she'd be up for a little surprise adventure this evening. The door to the shed was ajar, so he knocked lightly before pulling it fully open.

Summer sat on the floor, her notebook open as she intensely focused on moving her pen across the paper.

"What are you over there writing?"

She sniffed. Closing the book, she waved it at him mockingly. "This is called a diary for a reason. It's personal."

"Dear Diary, Alex Trebek is so hot!"

She giggled swiping away the tears she thought he hadn't seen. She tucked the diary back into her bag before looking at him. Her eyes roamed his body before concentrating on his face. Pointing a finger at him, she waved it randomly in his general direction. "You're up to something."

"How are you feeling today?"

She huffed in annoyance.

"Okay, I'm going to take that as an 'I'm feeling like my usual sassy self' type of good." He took a seat across from her. "I asked because I was hoping you might like to join me on a date tonight."

"Of course I would. But I'm not sure my mom's going to let me." She frowned. "Nurse Drill Sergeant is in full effect."

"What if I told you that I already took care of it?"

She perked up then. Dropping her hands to her cheeks, she squealed. "Really? Where are we going?"

He gave her a knowing look. "Now where would the fun be in just telling you everything right now?"

She groaned in mock complaint. "Always with the secret plans."

"All the better to surprise you with, O beautiful bossy one. Now come on, your mom is taking you out to get what you need for tonight and don't even think about asking her about tonight, she's sworn to secrecy. "

"I hate surprises."

Parker nodded. "I know. You'll survive."

"We're crashing a wedding?"

"Oh yeah. Your mom's going to be waiting for us with a getaway car if we have any trouble."

Summer giggled, leaning into him as they walked towards the entrance of the reception hall.

When he saw the item on her list, he knew it was one that he would make sure they crossed off, just for the reckless fun of it. But when things had gone the way they'd gone between the two of them, and he had learned more about all the experiences growing up with her condition had cost her, Parker knew it was a chance to make her feel special and loved before she'd have to go through another round of surgery and recovery before embarking on the hardest waiting period of her life. He had looked in the local papers for a few days until he found a wedding that would work.

It had all led up to today. With Kelly on board to help Summer get ready for the night, Parker had gone shopping in his father's closet, borrowing a suit that fit him perfectly. Summer's eyes had nearly fallen out of her head when she laid eyes on him.

He returned the reaction at the sight of her in the champagne colored, tulle dress that fell to just below her knees. Her hair had been elegantly twisted into an elaborate bun, small golden butterflies adorning it.

She was absolutely breathtaking.

The two of them had simply stared at each other in love and lust, while Kelly demanded pictures.

"Take one on my camera too please."

"And mine." Summer added.

He held his phone out, never taking his eyes off his one of a kind girl. He doubted he would ever forget the way she looked tonight but a picture would ensure it. He wanted to be able to look back one day and see the look of pure love on his face because that's what he was feeling in his heart right then.

The whole ride to the venue had been full of shy looks,

secret smiles, and gentle touches that promised more.

Stepping into the massive hall they immediately blended in with the crowd of wedding goers.

"How are we going to find seats? Aren't they always assigned?"

"Who said anything about sitting? I want a dance."

He had spent an entire evening planning this whole thing out just right. If his calculations were correct then they'd be walking just as the real party got underway, leading to a seamless entrance and transition onto the dance floor.

Parker led his date on the dance floor and held her close. They moved slowly, with Summer off her oxygen, he was careful not to over exert her.

"This must be what it feels like to go to prom."

"No, sweetheart, this is so much better. But you'll be able to tell me for yourself when I take you to my senior prom."

She looked up at him eagerly, "Yeah?"

"Yeah sweetheart. Homecoming, prom, and whatever other dances they do here, I'm bringing my girl."

He brought her hand to his lips and kissed her knuckles, pausing to admire how pretty his ring looked on her finger. It made his heart swell every time he saw it on her finger, which had been pretty much all the time since he gave it to her.

"I wish this dance could last forever."

"Me too."

Chapter Thirty One

Fresh out of the shower, Parker collapsed on to the mattress in his bedroom. True to his word, Luke had made sure he ordered Parker a proper bed and furniture for his new room. So, though his room was still primarily bare, it was far more comfortable. His clothes for the morning were all laid out on top of his dresser. Summer's early morning check in at the hospital meant an even earlier alarm setting on his phone, he didn't want to leave anything to chance.

Luke had already agreed to put a hold on registering him over at the high school until next week in order for him to stay by Summer's side as she began her recovery without accumulating any absences. He would have skipped the days regardless, but it was nice to have the permission up front.

His phone buzzing for attention, he grabbed it from the nightstand with one hand, unlocking it quickly with a well-practiced thumb.

Summer: Come outside

Checking the time on his phone, he pushed himself off the bed and grabbed a shirt before hurrying to see why on earth she was outside near midnight when she should have been resting.

She was indeed outside, sitting on an old quilt he was used to seeing in the corner of her shed. The crocheted blanket she often fell asleep with on the couch had been wrapped around her shoulders. Autumn was in the air that night.

"What on earth on you doing out here, Summer? You could get sick."

"I'm already sick, Parker."

"That's not what I meant." He sat down behind her, taking her to task about being outside.

"Are you done fussing yet?"

"Yeah, pretty much." He wrapped himself around her and relished the moment she leaned into him. She had loosed her hair from the braid she'd worn it in all day and as he held her, it fell across his arms in thick shiny waves.

"There are so many stars out tonight. I just wanted to feel their light on my skin."

He joined her then, tipping his head back to be struck with the starry sight. His mind drifted back to the night when she advised him to look up at those times when he was afraid of falling.

"I can't believe the summer is ending already. It feels like just yesterday you were spying on me through the kitchen window."

"For the last time, I wasn't spying! I was just observing...intensely."

Her giggle turned into a sigh. "You made me love you."

He kissed her neck, eliciting another breathy sigh. She smelled of sunshine, soap, and honey. It was the best smell in the world. "I'm pretty sure I've loved you since the beginning."

Her shoulders rose and fell with a heavy exhale. "You know every time I go into surgery, I end up losing something. A father, friends, my normalcy. I really don't want to lose anything this time."

"You won't." Parker hugged her a little harder. "Your mom and I, we're going to be there. I'm not going anywhere unless you're coming with me."

"Promise?" A tear rolled down her cheek.

"I swear it. Even Luke's gonna be around." He made a stricken face which produced another round of giggles from her.

Parker was waiting for Kelly and Summer at their car early the next morning. In the chill of the morning air, he'd pulled on a hoodie and sat sipping on a travel mug of hot coffee Luke had prepared for him. The sun hadn't made its appearance yet, but every so often you could hear the sounds of birds waking up ready to start their routine, as if this was some ordinary day.

As if.

She walked towards him in her oversized sweatshirt that fell down to the middle of her legging covered legs. One yellow Converse and one lime green one covered her feet. Her damp hair had brushed into a neat and tidy bun, and her face was free of any emotion. It was only as she drew closer did he spot the ear bud in her ear.

She flashed him a weak smile, taking his hand quietly and walking to the car. The ride to the hospital was quiet, the mood somber. Something told him that this is how Summer wanted it and neither he nor Kelly desired to force her to talk. His own nerves were kicking up as every minute took them closer to the hospital, but he forced himself to find peace in holding her hand and being there as an anchor of support.

Out of the blue, she extended an ear bud to him in silent invitation to join her. The sounds of stringed harmonies instantly filled his ear. He glanced at her to see just a tiny flash of a smile on her lips right before she closed her eyes. Parker did the same. He had never listened to classical music before, at least not the way Summer did. This time though, he wanted to hear what she heard. With his eyes closed he stopped listening for notes or instruments and instead listened for the story. The rise and fall of the music instantly took his mind away, the emotions behind each sound finally made sense.

As the song came to a close, so did their car ride. Kelly pulled the car into the parking garage of the hospital just as Summer turned off her phone. Giving his hand a squeeze, she spoke her first words of the day.

"Well, let's do this."

Parker helped carry her hospital bags into the room before relegating himself to the waiting room to wait for her to get through her pre-op work. He would get to see her just once more before she would be brought in and put under so he used the time alone to collect both his thoughts and emotions. He rested his elbows against his knees to try and keep them from nervously bouncing up and down.

Up until now, Parker hadn't allowed any negative thoughts to blossom. He wouldn't think about the worst-case scenario because it just wasn't an option to him. But sitting in this room by himself, his fight against those thoughts became overwhelming. Over the last week, he saw that dynamic energy of hers fall too quickly. The girl who had fearlessly tackled tasks had suddenly grown winded just walking up her front porch steps. He'd seen the exhaustion build up and threaten to wash her away.

"Parker?" Kelly's voice snapped him out of his own head. "She's ready for you."

He left his bag on his seat, walking over to Kelly and embracing her. If this was hard for him, he couldn't imagine what she was going through right now. He didn't know what to say, but a hug is something he could do. Her arms wrapped around him and squeezed. "Thank you, now you better hurry up before she comes marching out here herself."

"You're not coming?"

Kelly shook her head. "You go on and have your moment with her. I'll come back in a bit."

He followed Kelly's clear directions to her room, eager to see his girl, determined to say all the right things. When he stepped into the pre-op room, all he could do was look at her and take her in. Her clothes had been traded in for a hospital gown and her toe ring had been stripped from her toe. She smiled softly.

"Hey you."

"Hey yourself." He pressed a kiss to her hand, then her forehead, then her lips. It still wasn't enough.

She held out the ring, "I can't wear this in surgery. Will

you hold on to it for me?"

"Of course." He pressed a kiss to it, sliding it as far down his pinky finger as it would go. "So I was thinking that tomorrow, we need to get started on a new list. All the stuff to do this fall. I'm thinking apple picking is in order, we can go to the MET in New York on Thanksgiving break, anything you want."

"I'm glad you came, Parker."

"I told you I was going to be here every step of the way- "

She shook her head and interrupted him. "I'm not talking about the hospital. I'm glad you came to Concord."

Restricted emotions stung at the back of his eyes. He sat on the edge of the bed, needing to be as close to her as possible. "I'm glad I came too. It was the best punishment I ever got."

Her reddened eyes grew watery then. She sniffed as she fiddled with the ID bracelet on her wrist. "You're the best friend I've ever had."

A single tear escaped her eye. And then another. "Parker, if anything happens to me, if I don't make it…"

He pressed a desperate kiss to her lips. Desperate to taste her. Desperate to keep her words unsaid. The sweetness of her sigh melted under the weight of her tears. She brought her hand to his face, cradling his own wet cheek in her palm.

Not yet.

He wasn't ready yet.

"I love you, Summer."

Chapter Thirty Two

Time flies.

Except when you're waiting for any kind of update about your girlfriend who was having her chest opened and then put back together. Dr. York had informed them the procedure would take anywhere from four to six hours. After forty-five minutes he felt like he was going to lose his mind.

Two hours into it, he was nearly ready to explode. He didn't know how people did this.

"No news is good news in this situation."

Kelly reminded him as she sat with a bag of yarn at her feet and crochet needles in her hands. She offered to teach him how to do it, probably due to the fact that she was sick of his pacing. Aside from the comical relief the idea presented, Parker declined, knowing his hands were far too jumpy right now to do anything productive.

Three hours later: Luke had been updated. He had successfully cleared about twenty levels of Candy Crush, and he had listened to half of the playlist Summer had made for him.

By the time the clock hit the fifth hour, he needed to do something that felt useful. "Can I grab you a cup of coffee or anything?"

Kelly set her crochet needles down. "You know, a cup of tea would be nice. Do you know your way to the cafeteria?"

"No, but I'll find it. Finding food is one thing I'm good at."

Despite their worry they both exchanged hearty grins.

He found the cafeteria easily, proceeding to load up the cardboard tray with two cups of tea and a soda, throwing on several packaged pastries and chips before heading over to the register. Returning to the Family Waiting Room, Parker stepped off the elevator and turned down the hallway that would get him there.

Met with the sight of Kelly standing there talking with Dr. York made his blood run cold. And when Kelly sobbed, his limbs suddenly felt like they were made of cement. His chest throbbed...

Suddenly, Kelly was in front of him. Her hands on both of his shoulders, shaking him lightly.

"Parker! She's out of surgery!"

When Summer opened her eyes for the first time after surgery, Parker was there.

He and Kelly had hugged each other excitedly, talking to Summer in soft tones as she came out of anesthesia. Dr. York had been in again to check her stats, and to give Kelly a list of technical information, but Parker found it hard to concentrate on anything other than his girl. He linked her hand in his gingerly, mindful of her IV and his stitches.

"I know you're sleepy sweetheart but I know you're listening. I'm going to have to leave in a bit. Visiting hours for me are coming to a close, but I'm going to be back first thing in the morning and I'm going to bring you something special."

At first, he didn't know if she could hear him, but the squeeze of his hand told him otherwise. Leaving her after a day like today would be hard, but he held on to the fact that at least he was leaving with a whole lot of hope and a plan to see her in the morning.

He collected his bag from the chair. "If she wakes up tonight, please remind her I'll be back in the morning."

Kelly nodded lovingly. "I will. How are you getting home? Do you need to borrow our car? I'll be here all night and won't have need for it."

"My dad is waiting for me right now. Thanks for the offer though."

She crossed her arms over her chest. "Thank you for being here today. It was nice not to have to do this alone."

Parker hugged her for the hundredth time that day. "Thanks for allowing me to be here. I'll see you tomorrow morning."

"Until tomorrow then."

Chapter Thirty Three

He watched as she unwrapped the gold wrapping paper and revealed the special edition of Charlotte's Web. Her fingers gingerly traced the embossed lettering.

"It's beautiful. Thank you."

He admired her face. Her color was better today. The healthy pink was returning to her cheeks and a smile danced in her eyes. It was the most welcome sight in the world.

"Dr. York said you might be in here for a couple of weeks so I figured I would bring you a book every day to keep your mind sharp. I can't have my favorite teacher slipping, I'm going to need your smarts this year."

She really smiled then and put the book to the side.

"I can't eat what I want, I can't watch what I want. I'm already so bored. Distract me. When are you starting school?"

"Luke is going to register me this Friday. I'll start on

Monday."

She clapped. "I can't wait to hear all about it!"

"My mom is coming into town this weekend. She's going to be bringing a bunch of my clothes and stuff. I told her she could just mail it but she insisted on driving. I think she wants to check up on me and spy on Luke."

Summer's lopsided grin made him happy.

"She's going to be so proud of you."

He blew air out of the corner of his mouth. "I love my mom. I'm always going to. But the truth is I didn't do any of this for her."

She simply blinked because she knew.

"I was thinking that while my mom is here, I'd like her to meet you, if you think that'd be alright."

She glanced down at her chest for one self-conscious minute. "You don't think she'd be freaked out by all of this?"

"By how freakishly beautiful you are? Or by how freakishly smart you are?"

She giggled, accepting the soft kiss he placed on her lips. "There's nothing more she'd want to do than meet the girl who saved her delinquent son. You were the best thing to ever happen to my life, you know?"

Summer wrinkled her nose at him. "You love me and my robo-heart?"

"You bet your sweet heart I do."

Parker stayed with Summer until it was time for him to leave. With Luke's arrival to take him home, the worst part of the day had come. He hated saying goodbye to her, especially as her smile turned sad while she watched him collect his things.

"I wish I could go with you."

"Soon you will, so get some rest." He slid the straps of his backpack over his shoulders before leaning over and kissing her. "Call me before you go to bed, okay?"

"K." She squeezed his hand tightly. "I'll see you tomorrow?"

"I'll be here as soon as they let me."

He slid the door open to leave but paused, looking over his shoulder to get one more look at her to hold him over until the morning. His beautiful Summer with her messy bun lay looking at him with a depth of feelings in her eyes. He was instantly pulled back to her, pressing another urgent kiss to her lips, letting his mouth linger.

"You know I love you, right?"

She nodded, gently touching her ring that hung from the string around his neck. "I love you, too."

Chapter Thirty Four

"Are you hungry? I picked up a chicken."

Luke held up a plastic grocery bag before setting it on the kitchen counter.

"Was it heavy?" Parker chuckled at his own joke, laughing only harder when Luke's confused face proved he hadn't gotten it. He would have to tell Summer about it when they talked later. She would laugh.

"I ate a bit at the hospital but I'll probably be hungry again in a bit. I'll come down and grab some later."

Pulling a bottle of Gatorade out of the fridge he cracked the seal and took a gulp. "Mom texted to say she'd be coming in sometime Friday morning with my things."

Luke paused, his face paling for just a minute. "Should I be here? I mean, does she want to see me?"

He shrugged. "I wouldn't know. But I would guess, yes. I'm sure she'll want to warn you about all my irresponsible tendencies."

"Is that really how you think your mother feels about you?"

Another shrug. Another swallow.

Luke pulled his glasses from his face, carefully folding them before sliding them into his pocket. His eyes focused in on Parker. "I can't speak for your mother, but I can speak on what I've seen this summer. Whatever happened back in New York, it has no bearing on who you are. You've done so much these last few months that you should be proud of... that I *am* proud of."

Parker cleared the lump from his throat with a forcible cough. "I should get upstairs. I have some work to do."

"Okay Parks."

Luke adjusted the bag on his shoulder as he walked toward the steps. "Uh, Dad?"

"Yeah?"

"Thanks for the chicken."

Parker pulled his laptop onto his lap. He'd been mulling over the college essay questions for weeks now wondering which one would be the right one. He wasn't a writer. It had never been easy for him to put a pen to paper and write the way he felt. Somehow, getting into college had become important to him and now, with so much riding on this whole college application, he didn't want to screw it up.

He had thoughts of Summer getting through this year, getting her transplant and getting healthy enough to be by his side when they both started freshman year at some university. They would take spring break trips to places with palm trees, and spend their summers backpacking through Europe. He had thoughts of Summer.

They wanted to know about someone he admired, someone who influenced him to the point that his behavior and world view had shifted. There was only one answer for such a question.

He put his fingers to the keyboard and began to write.

An hour later, Parker jogged down the stairs with his stomach on his mind. Visiting the fridge, he gratefully pulled out the rotisserie chicken. Opening the dishwasher, he grabbed a clean fork, prepared to take both back upstairs to his room when his phone rang.

Summer's name illuminated the screen.

"Hey Sum-"

Kelly's wails interrupted him.

chapter Thirty Five

Summer died at 8:43 on a Thursday evening.

If anyone was paying attention they would have felt the world stop.

Silence eclipsed him.

The crickets and bull frogs had grown quiet, and the fireflies dimmed their lights.

The world stopped.

His world stopped.

Chapter Thirty Six

They had told him something about post-operative complications.

There was some kind of explanation involving a blood clot.

But none of the words made sense to Parker. Nothing anyone could say could explain how the girl he had just seen in recovery just a couple of hours ago was no longer alive. The surgery that was supposed to keep her around had taken her still.

No, he couldn't understand. He would never understand.

Rage throbbed in his heart; each beat driving him insane with grief. It was a searing pain. A pain only felt at the division of heart and soul; a pain worse than anything he'd ever felt. He screamed against the madness until his vocal cords protested. Luke again holding him in loving restraint, knowing there were never going to be any words to soothe this kind of pain. He lost track of how long he lay on the kitchen floor, his body racked with a soul-howling grief that seemed to have no end in sight.

It was a kind of pain where he despised the sun for rising the next morning. He cursed the birds for singing and the living for living. He hated the world for continuing on as if Summer wasn't dead.

Dead.

The word soured his stomach.

He lay in his room with the curtains drawn. His heart was afraid to catch a glimpse of anything that reminded him of her, knowing everything reminded him of her.

Luke's concerned knocking persisted even though he knew Parker wouldn't answer. His phone buzzed with calls and messages until the battery gave out. His eyes ached and he felt completely exhausted from how much crying he'd done. But then he would think about tomorrow and his broken heart would fill with fresh hurt. His mom would be here sometime in the next twelve hours and expect to see him. In the next few days, he would be expected to go back to school. He didn't know how he could deal with any of it. They would all tell him some terrible cliché about time healing all wounds or something similar. But no one would have any answers when he told them he didn't want to be seen and he didn't want to cope. And no one would answer when he asked how he could go on knowing he'd never see her face again.

His hand reached for the ring that still hung around his neck next to the key to her shed. He held on to her ring tightly, the memory of her birthday flashed before his eyes. The way her smile illuminated her whole face every time she looked at him was what he saw every time he closed his eyes now.

Quiet commotion from below is what stirred him out of his sleep.

The murmuring of voices and footsteps from below were making it hard for him to imagine the world away. Not bothering to look at his phone as he plugged it up to charge, he swung his feet to the edge of the bed and propelled himself towards the door.

He stood at the top of the stairs unmoving.

He knew once he went down there he would be surrounded by voices, and not one of them would be Summer's. He would give anything to walk into that kitchen and see her sitting there reading a book, ready to berate him for not being awake before the sun. His throat burned with emotion.

Parker walked down the stairs slowly, stepping into both the kitchen and the unwelcome sunlight at the same time. The sight of both of his parents in the same place immediately made him uneasy. Luke's face looked full of worry and exhaustion at the sight of him, while his mother's looked full of relief.

"Parker."

She crossed the tile and enveloped him into a hug he didn't want, but was everything he needed. Just yesterday he was telling Summer of his plans to introduce the two of them, and now no one would ever get that honor again.

"I think you grew since the last time I saw you."

Parker shrugged. "Maybe."

"I brought you a couple of breakfast sandwiches. Your dad said you hadn't eaten anything."

He shook his head grabbing a water from the refrigerator. The idea of eating made him nauseated. "Not hungry."

She reached out and put her hand on his arm. "You need to keep your strength up, P."

"For what?" He scoffed. "My girlfriend is dead, Mom. An egg sandwich isn't going to fix that."

Parker turned on his heel ready to flee, when a thought put a stop to his feet. Turning, he looked past Laura's face and into his father's. "Have you heard from Kelly?"

Luke nodded, shoving his hands into his pockets as he walked towards him. "She called about an hour ago. The funeral will be on Sunday."

His grip tightened on the bottle of water and he drew in a long inhale to steady himself.

"If you want to go over to visit Kelly, she's home now."

Parker shook his head adamantly. He couldn't go over to that house. Not yet. Maybe not ever again. "I'm just going to go upstairs."

Laura's call for him to wait fell on his back as he took the stairs two at a time. The last thing he heard was his father telling her to leave him be for a while.

Thank you, Luke.

Chapter Thirty Seven

He had never been to a funeral before.

He stood there between Luke and Kelly in his new black suit, a pair of new all black converses on his feet and his hands fisted at his side. As his eyes were focused on the casket draped in wildflowers, the strung ring he wore underneath his black dress shirt felt heavy against his chest.

Kelly's sniffles ignited a new wave of guilt. He hadn't spoken to her since the evening she called and broke his heart. Still when they arrived at the cemetery, he felt the need to be by her side as they both said good bye to the love of their lives.

Sometimes words weren't necessary, this was one of those times.

Scanning the crowd, he studied all the faces around Summer's casket. Some were fully of sympathy, some of empathy, but one... one was full of something Parker couldn't identify, at least not right away. The man had something familiar about him though Parker knew he hadn't met him before. When his brain caught up to his eyes, Parker knew exactly who and what he saw. Summer's guilty father.

He rolled his eyes at his presence. It made him angry on Summer's behalf, furious even. But he couldn't take a day like today and pile anymore negative emotions into the heart shaped void he felt. He gritted his teeth together as he listened to words spoken about his girl. The words he wanted to speak, lodged deep down under his grief. He bowed his head so he wouldn't have to see people who barely spoke to her sniff their way through the service.

Parker stayed put even as the rest of the crowd began to disperse. One by one, they walked by muttering some words of condolence in Kelly's general direction before leaving. Until it was just the two of them.

He watched as Kelly walked up to the casket and fell to her knees.

He turned his back to give her the deserved privacy when he spotted none other than Richie Gregory standing there in his funeral black. When he texted Richie in the middle of the night with the news, he hadn't kept his phone on long enough to read any responses. But he should have known that out of anyone, Richie would show up for him.

"You came."

"Of course I came." He gave Parker a light shoulder push. "You want to get out of here?"

Parker looked over his shoulder once more, his heart finding a new way to break every time he looked at that wooden box. Kelly stood and walked in the opposite direction into the waiting arms of a friend. Not answering Richie, he ran back over pressing a furious kiss to the polished wood of the casket before whispering his love one more time. He returned to Richie's side with tears burning his eyes. He slipped on his sunglasses.

"Let's go."

For about an hour, Richie drove them around in aimless directions before pulling into the driveway of Parker's house. He hadn't tried to get Parker to talk about Summer. He hadn't tried to fill the silence with random small talk aimed to distract him from the biggest loss he had ever felt. Richie did what every great friend would do. He understood.

"So…" He killed the ignition of the car and turning to face him. "You're staying in Concord."

"Leaving never felt right after falling in love with Summer."

"And now?"

Parker dug in for the words he needed to explain his feelings. "If I leave, I'm afraid of never feeling anything ever again. I can't do that, Rich. I don't want to not feel Summer. If I have to hurt every day to make sure I remember her, then I'll take the pain."

Laura stepped out onto the front porch then interrupting their conversation. She held up a hand, to which Parker nodded. He was being summoned. With a grateful goodbye to Richie and a promise to check in, Parker exited the car. As he walked up the driveway towards his mom, he purposely didn't look across the lawn to the neighboring house.

"I'm going to have to get on the road soon and I wanted to talk to you for a minute."

Parker loosened his tie sitting on the porch step. "Thanks for staying for the funeral."

Laura sat next to him, pulling him over and planting an effusive kiss to his cheek. "I'm sorry there even was a funeral. But I'm happy I could be here for you."

Parker popped the knuckles on his hand. "You would have really liked her."

"I know I would have. It takes a special kind of girl to love you Reeves boys." She flashed him a tender smile. "I'd love to hear about her, when you're ready to share."

He nodded. He couldn't imagine a time where talking about loving and losing Summer wouldn't feel like he was ripping his heart out, but it was nice to think about for the minute.

"You sure you want to stay?"

He gave his mother the smallest of smiles. "I'm sure."

A teary smile and a sniff came from her as she wrapped him in her arms. "I love you so much, P. I only want the best for you. I'm going to miss you."

"I know. I love you, Ma."

Chapter Thirty Eight

It had been two weeks since they buried Summer. Since then, he finally put his back pack on his back and headed off to start his senior year. The monotony of a school schedule kept him from wanting to lock himself away in his misery. Monday through Friday he lived life on repeat. He would focus on the mundane simplicity of getting through each Summer-less task one at a time.

During the school day, he moved through the hallways like a shell of a person. Every so often he would try to smile back at the new friendly faces that tried to welcome him to the school but none of the smiles felt like her smile. There would never be another Summer smile.

Every time it hit him, it was like a frigid air infiltrated his lungs, causing them to seize up and threatening to take his breath away.

By the time the weekend arrived, Parker felt exhausted with the exertion of trying to find his footing in her absence. For a few brief moments on Friday afternoon he would feel grateful that he wouldn't have to wear a mask for anyone.

Then, he'd start thinking of the could-have-been weekend plans and he would once again be thoroughly consumed with missing his best friend.

That particular day, he looked out the window of his kitchen, for the first time being able to look at her shed without completely falling apart. He fingered the key that still hung from his neck along with her ring, his attention only pulled away when he spotted Kelly dragging out her recycling bins.

Guilt pangs struck again. He knew it was time to talk to her. With his heart pounding with emotion, he pulled open his door and took the well-traveled path over to her yard. Spotting his approach, she paused her task and offered a watery smile.

Once he was in arms reach, he took a breath that made his chest shudder.

"Hey, Kelly? I just want to say sorry, you know, for staying away after the funeral and everything. I just didn't know how to come over here and not see her. I miss her so much it hurts. But I still should have come to see you…"

Kelly took his hands in hers squeezing them for a moment. "No apology needed. I understood."

"Even if the apology isn't needed, it's owed. You welcomed me into your home and your lives and never showed me anything but love. I want you to know if you need anything, even if you just want someone to talk about her with, I'm always going to be here for you."

Kelly hugged him then. It was one the best hugs in the world; the kind of hugs that they must teach all mothers how to give. The kind that makes you feel loved down to your toes.

"You know, the first time I saw you on our doorstep, I knew you would be important to her. I saw the way you two looked at each other, and I knew. You gave her something magical, Parker. She loved you."

"I loved her the same. I always will."

Kelly released him holding him by the shoulders. "I hope you'll come by and raid my refrigerator every few days."

He managed a smile. "I can do that."

"I bumped into Luke the other morning. I was wrestling with my trash cans and he helped me out. He mentioned you were getting ready to send in your college applications. I'm so proud of you."

"Yeah. I figured the earlier I get started the better." He cleared his throat nervously. "I'm thinking of a pre-med track. Maybe pursuing a future in pediatric cardiology..."

He felt dumb saying it out loud. Kelly smiled softly, pursing her lips the same way Summer used to. "You're going to need a quiet place to study and keep your grades up then. I want you to feel free to use Summer's shed. I haven't touched it since, it didn't feel right. It was always her space. She chose to share it with you and so I think she would want you to have it now."

His hand instinctively went to the key she'd given him. "Thanks, Kelly."

Parker slid the key into the lock, turning it smoothly. His hand on the knob, he hesitated. He hadn't been in this room since his last time with Summer. He wondered if her sweet smell would still fill the air, if he would be able to feel her in the memories they'd shared. An image of her sun kissed and barefoot as she lay writing on the floor played behind his eyelids as he squeezed them shut.

Blowing out a shaky breath, he entered the room. Instant emotion clawed at his chest as he closed the door behind him, his eyes fixed on the board full of snap shots of their summer. He loved every single one of those pictures. Each one of them evoking a memory; each memory full of smiles. Full of her.

His eyes drifted to wear her camera still hung and saw something that made his blood run cold. A simple rectangular envelope with one simple word written in familiar loopy cursive writing. *Parker.*

He pulled the envelope free from the tape holding it in place, turning it over in his hands. Summer had written him and he had no idea what she was going to say. It made his heart race with anticipation. He sat in the bean bag chair and ran his fingers over the pen strokes of his name.

Parker slowly opened the envelope, wanting to preserve as much of it as he could. Pulling out the piece of lined paper and a flash drive, he set the envelope to the side.

Tears had filled his eyes as he began to read.

Dear Parker,

Writing this letter has been the hardest thing I've ever written because if you're reading this it means things didn't work out the way we wanted them to.

I'm hoping I got a chance to tell you no matter what happens I'm so happy.

Thank you for giving me the best summer of my life. You were the best friend I could have ever imagined, and somehow I got lucky enough to call you my boyfriend. I can't imagine how I would have gotten through this summer without you. I don't want to imagine it.

I guess you might be curious to what's on the flash drive. Remember the little item on the list about writing a letter to the random stranger? Well on that little flash drive there's a letter to the admission offices of your choice. A recommendation letter to be more precise. I know the idea of your deceased seventeen-year-old girlfriend writing you a recommendation is a little (a lot) weird, but no one knows you like I know you, Parker.

I know you're the type of guy who is loyal to his

friends even when they aren't loyal to him. You're loyal even to the point of risking your own reputation and good name (don't do this anymore by the way!). You're good, one of the best people I've ever met. You're a man of your word.

Guess what? You're smart and responsible.

You're also the best kisser ever. Don't worry, I didn't put that part in the letter.

I hope I got to tell you that I loved you and I hope you heard me. I love you Parker, more than I ever knew I could. You were the first person who saw me for me and not for my condition, and you loved me still. You made me want to make plans.

Don't stop making plans, Parker.

Make plans and follow through. Do whatever you set your mind on. Make a difference.

And if along the way, an episode of Jeopardy

comes on or you decide to play on a slip and slide in the rain. I hope you'll think of the girl next door with the red hair and smile.

My heart hurts to think of leaving you, but I'm finally resting now.

Oh, and one last thing Ride the Ferris wheel Ride it and feel And if the fear of falling gets to be too much, look up.

Love,

Summer Raines

P.S. Take care of Mom for me

Parker pressed the letter to his lips kissing her words again and again as his tears came. It felt like he could breathe again for the first time in weeks. Summer's love had stained his soul. The tapestry of his DNA would be forever changed because of the few months she'd shone her light into the darkest corners of his heart and his life.

Summer would always be the love of his life.

He knew there would be days where he would remember her and miss her so fiercely it would make it feel nearly impossible to think about living without her.

But no matter what he would go on and try his absolute best to live a life in a way that would have made her proud.

Folding the letter back carefully, his eyes caught sight of another piece of paper in the envelope. He pulled it out with a smile. She had given him her list. With all the activities crossed out he couldn't help but to chuckle. It had been an adventure falling in love with her. Turning the paper over to the back, he was surprised to see the addition of four items she hadn't shared with him before.

A sob broke free from his chest as he pressed a fist to his mouth, allowing himself to feel whatever came.

Not bothering to wipe his eyes free of the tears clouding his vision, he stood and made his way over to the cork board where he removed a picture taken of the two of them together. He ran his thumb over her sweet face, those cinnamon freckles still having their usual effect and making him smile.

His beautiful summer girl...

Taking the picture, he grabbed a notebook and a pen from her desk.

Settled on the floor, he pulled his phone from his pocket and few quick swipes of his thumb brought up his playlist. Pressing play on Vivaldi's *Summer,* he waited for the orchestra to come to life before he opened the notebook to a blank page.

A tear ran down his cheek as he began to write.

Dear Summer ...

Summer's Bucket List

~~Meet someone new~~

~~Climb a tree~~

~~Ride a bike~~

~~Try a new food~~

~~Do something crazy just for fun~~

~~Go to a drive in~~

~~Eat Funfetti pancakes~~

~~Play in the sprinklers~~

~~Visit a museum/art gallery~~

~~Get a fake ID~~

~~Be brave~~

~~Star Gaze~~

~~Catch Fireflies~~

~~Release Fireflies~~

~~Go to a concert~~

~~Go strawberry picking~~

~~Go swimming and wear a bikini~~

~~Make a difference~~

~~Send a letter to a random address~~

~~Volunteer~~

~~Get a tattoo~~

~~Crash a wedding~~

~~Help someone~~

~~Build a sand castle~~

~~Watch fireworks~~

~~Win a prize at the fair~~

~~Do something that scares you~~

~~First kiss~~

~~Fall in love~~

~~Make sure Mom will be alright~~

~~Say Goodbye~~

Acknowledgements

Dear Readers,

When I was about eighteen weeks pregnant with my twins, I walked into a routine ultrasound appointment only expecting to leave with new pictures of my growing babies and the news of what color clothes I could start buying. By the end of the appointment I had learned three things: I was having one girl, one boy... and my son had a congenital heart defect that would require surgical correction as soon as he was born.

I cried. A lot.

I was absolutely terrified for the safety of my baby. I wanted to stay pregnant forever, knowing that my heart was literally keeping his safe. But almost as quickly as I broke down, I had to build myself up. *Nothing is going to happen to my son* became my new daily mantra.

One surgery and seven and half years later, my son is a brave, bold, Batman-loving, energy driven little boy. He is strong, he is fearless, and I love his sweet heart. The scar that stretches across his ribs fades a bit more every year but the memory of his first battle of life is etched into my heart forever.

Every time I have to visit the hospital and have his cardiologist give us the thumbs up sign, I often stop and look around the massive waiting room. It's kind of impossible not to remember how your own child has been blessed in his recovery when you are surrounded by children of all ages dealing with an even more difficult CHD journey. I never forget. I am always grateful.

This story caused me many tears, lots of sleepless nights, and a whole lot of inner turmoil as I struggled to make sure I told this story the way the characters demanded it be told (and believe me, I tried to find any way around some of the most difficult parts of writing this one).

Summer's journey was part of Parker's story. Her journey may not have been easy or as long as one would want, but her journey --- just like every one of those kids in hospitals all over the world--- is one that is full of impact.

Thank you for reading.

Thank you to the readers who waited patiently as I did my best to get this story out the way I envisioned it. Every time one of you takes a chance on one of my books, my heart grows a hundred fold. I appreciate every one of you.

To all the nurses I peppered with questions and scenarios as I wrote, thank you for your patience and for the job you do daily.

To my cover designer at Recreatives: You captured the essence of my vision so perfectly. This cover was especially important to me. As soon as I got the idea of Parker's story, I saw a vision of what the cover would look like. I wanted a cover that would catch a heart even more than it would catch an eye, and that's exactly what I got.

To all the members of my Sweethearts group, thank you for making my Facebook days so much brighter with your sweet comments.

Kaitie, thank you for your eagle eye beta skills. I am so grateful and happy that our paths crossed. You're amazing and incredible, and I'm sorry I made you cry!

Keyanna, thanks isn't a big enough word for you. Thank you for your unending confidence in me. I had countless rough moments during this one and you kept my spirits high. I can't seem to say it enough, I appreciate you and your friendship so much.

To my children, I've always loved you and I always will.

XO,

Santana

Also by Santana Blair

Paradise Cove Series

And She Called Him Romeo

Thirty Days in Technicolor

Twice Upon a Time

To be notified of all new releases you can join my mailing list!

www.SANTANABLAIR.com

About The Author

Santana Blair lives in Connecticut with her husband and three kids.

She enjoys long walks through bookstores and stationery aisles. Her personal philosophy is that rainy days are perfect for getting lost in a good book. She's a sucker for a good love story.

When she's not reading or writing, she enjoys music, movies, and relaxing with family.

Santana loves connecting with fellow readers via social media.

Website ~ www.santanablair.com/

Facebook ~ www.facebook.com/authorsantanablair

Twitter ~ www.twitter.com/santanawrites

Instagram ~ www.instagram.com/authorsantanablair

Goodreads ~ www.goodreads.com/SantanaBlair

Made in the USA
San Bernardino, CA
08 March 2018